She Heard The Quiet Unlatching Of The Door.

Bree thought she imagined the click of a key in the lock. The night was dark and the room was layered in shadows. She couldn't see anything and assured herself that the sounds were in her imagination. After all, how could Simon be sleepwalking again?

But he was. One of the shadows moved, and she caught a reflection of his sandy hair in the moonlight. Before she could open her mouth, his hip depressed the mattress near her.

He leaned close and slid the palms of his hands into her hair. He ran his fingers through her tousled curls. It felt good. So wonderfully good that for a quick second, she almost gave in. Almost.

"Look, *cher*, this is *loufoque, zinzan, maboul*. Or in any language on earth, bonkers. Now stand up and walk back downstairs to your *own* bed."

He had listened to specific instructions before when he'd done this. But tonight, her words were worth a wooden nickel....

Dear Reader,

Welcome to Silhouette Desire! Naturally, I think you've made a spectacular choice because, for me, each and every Silhouette Desire novel is a delightful, romantic, unique book. And once you start reading your selection I *know* you'll agree!

Silhouette Desire is thrilling romance. Here you'll encounter the joys and even some of the tribulations of falling in love. You'll meet characters you'll get to know and like... and heroes you'll get to know and *love*. Sensuous, moving, compelling, these are all words you can use to describe Silhouette Desire. But remember, words are not enough—you must *read* and get the total experience!

And there is something wonderful in store for you this month: *Outlaw*, the first in Elizabeth Lowell's WESTERN LOVERS series. It tells the story of rough-and-tough Tennesee Blackthorne... a man of fiery passions and deep emotions.

Of course, *all* of February's Silhouette Desire books are terrific—don't miss a single one! Until next month...

All the best,

Lucia Macro
Senior Editor

JENNIFER GREENE

NIGHT LIGHT

SILHOUETTE *Desire*®

Published by Silhouette Books New York

America's Publisher of Contemporary Romance

SILHOUETTE BOOKS
300 East 42nd St., New York, N.Y. 10017

NIGHT LIGHT

ISBN: 0-373-05619-2

First Silhouette Books printing February 1991

Books by Jennifer Greene

Silhouette Desire

Body and Soul #263
Foolish Pleasure #293
Madam's Room #326
Dear Reader #350
Minx #366
Lady Be Good #385
Love Potion #421
The Castle Keep #439
Lady of the Island #463
Night of the Hunter #481
Dancing in the Dark #498
Heat Wave #553
Slow Dance #600
Night Light #619

Silhouette Intimate Moments

Secrets #221
Devil's Night #305
Broken Blossom #345

Silhouette Books

Birds, Bees and Babies 1990
''Riley's Baby''

JENNIFER GREENE

lives on a centennial farm near Lake Michigan with her husband and two children. Before writing full-time, she worked as a personnel manager, college counselor and teacher.

Ms. Greene has won many awards for her category romances, and was most recently named a winner of the RWA Rita award and the *Romantic Times* Best Series Author of 1988-1989. She has also written as Jeanne Grant.

One
***

Bree was experienced at getting lost. It was something she did often and well. Back country roads had a thousand times more flavor than a turnpike, and if an occasional wrong turn had landed her in some tight spots, she never minded. Usually, it paid to be impulsive. Life was no fun without a little risk, a little tempting fate, a little spin on the roulette wheel.

Tonight, though, just a bit, just a tad, just a smidgen...she was starting to feel scared—stomach-dropping, heart-thudding, cold-fingers scared.

A slash of lightning knifed the road straight ahead of her. The ensuing growl of thunder made her aging Volkswagen shake. Rain splattered on the windshield so blindingly hard that the squeaking wipers couldn't keep up. The sky was as black as a cave—not surprising, considering that the hour neared midnight—and the gravel road was turning into a mud-slick washout. A driver with any brains would get off the road.

Bree was *dying* to get off the road, but the lightning storm literally surrounded her. Pulling off was no solution; she'd only be more vulnerable. For the past hour, she kept thinking the storm would pass. It didn't. She kept thinking there would be a place—a motel, a gas station, a house—where she could pull over. There wasn't.

Another cascade of lightning bolts lit up the sky, revealing the desolate landscape of South Dakota's Badlands. By the storm's light, the country looked as eerie and alien as a moonscape. Rocks shaped like monoliths jutted in jeweled colors under the bath of lightning. The bleak land stretched for miles, punctured by wrinkled hills and sharply creviced ravines—but there was no sign of life.

It wasn't a land for the tame at heart, but no one had ever accused Bree Reynaud of being timid. She'd wandered into Badlands National Park late that afternoon and promptly fell in love. Huge dark clouds had begun clustering around sunset. She'd seen them; she'd known the storm was coming, but seeking shelter had been the last thing on her mind. The building storm had made the wild, lonely landscape come alive with breathtaking color. The view had been awesome, unforgettable.

She didn't regret seeing it. There were simply a few times in her life when she wished her dad's lectures had had some effect. Raoul Reynaud had done everything but stand on his head to drill caution into his youngest child.

Nothing, unfortunately, had worked.

The windshield steamed up again. Bree leaned forward to swipe it with the last of her tissues, and for those few seconds she had only one hand on the steering wheel. The tires chose that moment to barrel into a pool of water. When her VW bug skidded, she muttered a litany of Cajun swear words. By the time she won control of the car, her palms were so wet they could barely grip the wheel.

Okay, she wasn't a little scared. She was *damned* scared. She was also stopping at the first place that offered shelter. A cave would do. *Anything* would do.

Another slash of lightning streaked so close she could smell it. Its sister roar of thunder made her ears ring. Not that she was superstitious, but she came from a Louisiana bayou. Maybe this was an omen.

Maybe it was time she quit roving.

Maybe it was time for a twenty-seven-year-old woman to stop taking daredevil risks and pick up the reins of her life.

Maybe you'd better concentrate on just staying alive for now, Reynaud, she told herself. She cranked open a window. Needles of cold spring rain immediately poured through the crack, soaking the left sleeve of her red sweater, but there was no help for it. Without outside air the windshield steamed out of control. The wipers swiped a slush of rain from the glass... and suddenly she saw them—a clutch of bulky dark shadows.

She eased on the brake and backed up for another look. There were definitely some buildings a few hundred yards off the road. She turned and abruptly discovered that the cow path of a driveway was as traversable as a mud slide, but she didn't care. Shelter was shelter. Gold wouldn't look this good to an alchemist.

By the time she braked at the end of the long driveway, though, relief had turned to disbelief. This was ranch country. Ergo, she assumed she'd stumbled across a ranch house. The few spare buildings flanking the house could well be barns—it was too dark and stormy to see clearly—but the dwelling itself looked like Dracula's castle.

A tasteless Dracula's castle. Possibly the building may have blended into an Alps setting, but it simply looked silly in the middle of the Badlands. The dark gray stone stretched three pompous stories, liberally decorated with gothic turrets and fancy leaded-glass windows. Two squat stone lions bordered the massive front doors—neither particularly artistic, just big— and the yard was an unmowed prairie, no bushes or trees, just weeds.

At best, Bree thought, it was the home of an eccentric fruitcake. She dragged her purse strap to her shoulder, yet hesitated before opening the car door. She wasn't afraid, but she was definitely exhausted. Did she or didn't she have the energy left to tackle a fruitcake?

Another razor of lightning lit up the sky, and she climbed out of the car making rash mental bargains with God. She'd be careful for the rest of her life, she'd be cautious, she'd be good . . . if the fruitcake would just let her camp for the night in one of his barns.

She grabbed her denim jacket and raced the twenty steps to the front door. Even in that short distance, her hair was soaked before she could bang on the weathered oak doors.

Lights reflected through the windows on each side of the door, but no one answered. She banged on the door again, then tried the knob. Locked.

She banged again, louder, harder. Rain ran down her brow, clung to her eyelashes like webs, dampened her lips. She had to look like a drowned rat, which normally wouldn't bother her. Her figure was no great shakes, although she'd inherited the dark hair, blue eyes and magnolia skin of her Cajun ancestors. Striking looks were no asset to a woman traveling alone. Tonight she just wished she looked more respectable than a drenched waif.

Still no answer. She gave the doors one last pounding try... and nearly fell into the hall when the door jerked open.

Her speech was all ready—apologies for bothering him, a request for shelter of any kind. She'd stay in a barn; she'd stay anywhere. She wasn't a thief, she was only lost. She'd pay him.

The speech was spring ready, but the verbal horses refused to leave the barn. She'd been so positive the house owner would be a wizened old Mr. Eccentric.

The man glowering at her was neither wizened nor old, and he could have stepped right off of Wall Street. In the middle of ranch country, he was wearing suit pants, leather loafers and a classic button-down shirt neatly tucked in. The hour was midnight; he was still in a tie. Bree wondered briefly if he went to bed with his briefcase and was fascinated on sight.

She'd run across her share of characters on her travels, but rarely a *gros chien*—a big shot, in bayou lingo. More relevant, her unwilling benefactor could have been intimate kin to the granite lions on the front porch.

He was good-looking in a rough way—not that anyone would notice. A scowl looked permanently embedded in his broad forehead. He was built long and lean. Tawny hair framed a rectangular face that was all sharp edges—angular cheekbones, a jutting nose and a hard, square chin. He had the character lines of a man who took charge and kept it. No humor. No softness. His eyes were a wonderful dark charcoal gray—shrewd, intelligent eyes—but so hard. And again like the granite lions, he looked ready to chew on any lambs crossing his path.

Bree had always been insatiably curious about people. He clearly never suffered that problem. His gaze whipped the dripping length of her, and his sole response was a pithy "Hell." His hand shot out, and a second later the door slammed behind her with the echoing cadence of a tomb being closed.

Possibly she was less than welcome.

She considered hightailing it back to the lightning storm, but the shadowed hall was warm and dry. However nasty the lion, he was apparently offering her shelter. She summoned her most trustworthy smile and extended a hand. "My name is Bree Reynaud, Mister...?"

"Simon. Courtland."

She nodded. He probably hadn't noticed her hand. "Mr. Courtland, I'm terribly sorry to—"

"Don't bother telling me the story," he said impatiently. "It's obvious you were stranded by the storm.

How or why doesn't make any difference now. Stay there. I'll be right back."

He stalked off, muttering something about "all I need" and "what more could go wrong." Bree pushed the wet hair out of her eyes, staring after him. Spare minutes later he was back and efficiently piled a blanket, then a towel, then a button-down shirt in her arms.

She couldn't imagine what the button-down shirt was for, until she realized he was giving her something to sleep in. It was more than she expected in the way of hospitality—and she would have expressed her gratitude, if he'd just given her a chance.

"The place has been closed up for months—it's barely livable—but you'll have to settle for what you've got," he said irritably. "The downstairs is laid out like an *L*. Past a living room and an office is a den. The couch makes into a bed that's harder than nails."

"Honestly, I don't mind—"

"In the west wing, past a dining room and kitchen, is the bathroom. Get yourself in a hot shower before you get pneumonia. You'll have to use radiators to dry your clothes. There's a clothes dryer, but it doesn't work."

"That's fine, I—"

"If you're concerned about your privacy, don't be. I'm working upstairs. Stay away from the stairs and we'll get along fine. Now what about your car?"

"My car?"

"Is it in a ditch?"

"No, I—"

"Is it stalled somewhere?"

She wasn't quite sure why she felt so out of breath when he was the one snapping orders and questions faster than a general. "No, my car's running. I just couldn't keep going because of the—"

"Because of the storm, yes, obviously. I'm sure the details are very interesting." His tone said otherwise. "As long as your car's operable, I assume you'll have no problem being gone before I wake up. Leave things as you found them, and we'll call it square. If you have any other questions, let's settle them now."

Bree said, "There's nothing," and couldn't resist an irrepressible, "sir."

He missed her attempt at humor, which seemed the only thing he'd missed so far. His dark gaze had examined and probed every inch of her—not the way a man studies a woman, but the way a scientist classifies a glob under a microscope. Bree tried to remember the last time a man had treated her like your basically annoying glob. Although Simon couldn't know it, his attitude was wonderfully reassuring. If his taste had run toward wet brunettes, the situation could have been tricky.

That obviously wasn't going to be a problem.

"I assume you're traveling alone," he said testily.

"Yes." She thought that was obvious but evidently not to him.

"Tell me now if you plan to sneak in a critter—man or beast—from the back of your car."

"You have my word, *cher.* No felines, canines, or parasitic man friends stashed in the trunk of my VW," she said gravely.

He shot her a sharp look, and for the briefest moment she thought he was going to crack a smile, but no. Nothing was going to crack those granite features, and apparently when Mr. Courtland ran out of orders, he was all through talking. Behind him, a worn oak staircase was divided into two landings. He said "Good night," turned his back and climbed the stairs.

Bree stared after him even after he'd disappeared from sight. She was still drenched and dripping, yet oddly she felt overwarm instead of chilled. For no reason at all, her pulse was skidding, her heart bucking hard.

There was no question that he was a disturbing man. His abrasiveness, his rudeness hadn't bothered her. He had no reason to be welcoming to an unwanted nuisance of a visitor, but she'd seen the gaunt, drawn lines of exhaustion in his face. She had the impression of a man pushed to the edge, a pressure cooker left on high too long. Even a rigid authoritarian type could remember how to smile. Who kicked the life out of you, *cher?*

She closed her eyes and mentally sighed. It was a bad habit—caring. Simon's problems, of course, were none of her business—or likely to be.

Abruptly, she pushed off her squishy-damp sneakers and went searching for the shower. The antiquated bathroom with its ghastly purple tiles was directly off the kitchen. In short order, she stripped off her wet clothes and climbed under the pelting hot spray.

A few minutes later, clean, warm and dry, she pulled on Simon's shirt in front of the tiny steamed-up mirror. Although she was a respectable five foot five, the shirt sagged inches off her shoulders and had to be cuffed three times before she could see her hands. Mr.

Courtland was one tall kahuna, and she'd expected the fabric to be as stiff and abrasive as its owner. Instead, the fine linen was a caress on her bare skin.

Maybe he was a closet sensualist, she thought dryly, and tried an experimental yawn. It was a joke. The shower should have relaxed her, and heaven knew she was exhausted, but it was the wrong kind of tired. She was still wired from driving through the lightning storm and had glimpsed just enough of the house to whet her nosiness.

She found the den, where she was supposed to sleep, and spread out her wet clothes on a radiator. Then, tiptoe quiet, not risking a light except for the central hall fixture, she started exploring.

It wasn't his house. It couldn't be. Bree wasn't quick to peg people, but Simon was so obviously and unbendingly computer age. There were no chrome or space or sterile surfaces here, and he clearly hadn't been in the place long enough to unpack a suitcase of clothes, much less open the place up.

The crazy old house was a spine-tingling environment for ghosts and wild imaginations. Floorboards creaked. Wind whistled through cracks. The ceilings were draped with cobwebs, and dust sheets covered cluttered mountains of old furniture—couches with big clawed feet, tables with doilies and knickknacks, lamps with dangling glass prisms.

The only room she found locked was the office. The others were full of treasures. The living room floor was covered by a thick, luxurious, hundred-year-old Oriental rug. The kitchen had a hearth taller than a man, a brick oven on the side of the chimney and a pantry that a cook would die for. The dining room had an old-fashioned rope-and-pulley-rigged dumb-waiter.

She loved it—*all* of it. Including the chime clock that struck an ear-ringing one o'clock from under the ghostly folds of a white dust cloth and nearly scared her out of her mind. That put an end to her exploring. There was too much risk of her host hearing strange sounds and coming down to investigate. She hustled herself into the den and closed the door.

She'd already discovered that the overhead light switch didn't work, but there was a lamp by the couch. The book-lined den had a stone fireplace and smelled of old leather, dust and pipe smoke. When she pulled out the bed, she found, as Simon had warned her, that the mattress was harder than rock. It didn't matter. She'd slept on far worse. She switched off the lamp, wrapped herself in the blanket and snuggled in.

The darkness was absolute, and the trapped wind made eerie, moaning sounds in the chimney. The mattress creaked when she shifted onto her side. Lightning illuminated unfamiliar shadows, and a hard, cold rain was still sluicing down the windows.

Bree closed her eyes, yet sleep eluded her. The house had a good aura—a little ghostly, a little haunted, but overall the atmosphere was wonderfully warm and safe. It wasn't the house that kept her awake. It was the loneliness.

Too many strange beds. Too many unfamiliar places. A year without a hook to hang her hat, a year of being footloose and heart free and maybe—so her family fussed—reckless. Family was everything where she came from. At last count, she had some two hundred close relatives. All of them drummed the same beat: a twenty-seven-year-old woman should be settled down, preferably married with a baby in the oven or at least with a steady career.

A year before she'd been driven by the challenge and adventure of roving the country. In the beginning, it had been wonderful. Christmas on the South Carolina coast, spring in the Smokies, summer in Maine. Big cities, small towns, mainline America and all the fringes, different people, different life-styles—she'd lustily soaked in every experience.

It couldn't last forever, though, and even from the start Bree had known she was running...and exactly what she was running from.

Matthew hadn't been her first mistake, but he was the straw that broke the camel's back. She was tired of being a sucker. If someone needed her, she came running. Giving came naturally to her; so did trust. When you laid out your heart like a rug, there was always some man willing to walk all over it. And when a woman found herself making a pattern of the same mistakes, she'd damn well better do something to change.

Traveling alone had forced her to toughen up, learn to protect herself and develop better judgment. Self-reliance and self-sufficiency weren't innate character traits but rather skills a woman could learn. She had learned.

So why are you still on the road, Reynaud? she asked herself.

Bree sighed, punched the pillow and determinedly curled up tight. Tomorrow, she'd think about whys. Tonight, it was too late and too dark, and the long, exhausting day was fast catching up with her. Her limbs grew leaden and a murky sleepiness started to seep into her consciousness. Just before her lids drooped down, she was vaguely aware that she hadn't locked the door.

The thought made her smile. She might be impulsive, but she'd never been nuts. If she'd been stuck for the night alone with any other stranger, her first impulse would have been to check for a lock on the door. Not here. Simon had looked her over good and with about the same desire he'd show a dead dog.

She was safe... in fact, it occurred to Bree that she hadn't felt this secure, this luxuriously safe, in more than a year. And on that thought, she fell asleep.

In the middle of a dream, Bree's eyes suddenly blinked open. She'd slept an hour, maybe two. She was lying on her side with her arms bunched around a pillow, the way she always fell asleep. She was not, however, accustomed to waking with a man's long arm hooked around her waist and her fanny neatly tucked against a pair of hard thighs.

She would have let out a healthy, blood curdling scream if all the air wasn't momentarily locked in her lungs. Fear was a paralyzing emotion.

Fear didn't exactly disappear, but it changed into a more handleable emotion when she realized no one was attacking her. Or even trying. The male body curled against her was as heavy as dead weight. Warm, breathing, limp, dead weight.

She had the air in her lungs to scream now, but she was far more tempted to swear. After all this time of living on the road, Bree thought she'd honed her instinct for man trouble down to a fine art.

Obviously, it didn't pay to become too complacent, because she'd certainly bombed on this one.

She jerked onto her back, which effectively dislodged the blanket covering her, but had no effect on her sleeping Lothario. The tawny head simply nuzzled closer. Simon's hand groped and found the curve of her breast. Familiarly. As if he'd already come to know the shape and size of her right breast quite well.

She could have told him it wasn't any big deal.

Actually, he must have come to the same conclusion or he wouldn't have fallen asleep.

Not funny, Reynaud. The storm had stopped battering the windows, and the room was disturbingly soundless. Pale rays of moonlight came through the windows. She could see, but she was still too groggy to think clearly—not that she needed to think. There was nothing tricky about the situation. She had two obvious choices: either let him have it verbally or wake him with a nice, fat, stinging slap.

She voted for the slap, but then there was the problem of delivering it. Lying flat on her back, tangled in his shirt and the blanket and trapped beneath the weight of his arm, she lacked swinging leverage.

She pushed herself to a half-sitting position. Simon's hand reflexively dropped—actually it slid—intimately to her lap. Her gaze flew to his face. Startled, she realized his eyes were open.

He was awake.

Only not exactly.

Bree pushed a hand through her tumbled mass of hair. The stranger she'd met last night had been a dictatorial *gros chien* with cold, passionless, gunmetal-hard gray eyes. The lean, muscled build was the same, and the strong, striking features hadn't changed. But the man lying next to her had sensual eyes, dark and luminous with emotion, and they were focused directly on her face.

Only not exactly.

She waved a hand. He didn't blink. She touched his arm. His skin was cold, terribly cold, and she abruptly noticed that he wasn't wearing a damn thing but a pair of navy boxers. Sexual awareness shimmered through her nerves, unwanted and shamefully inappropriate. She ignored his obvious state of arousal, just as she tried to ignore his smooth, muscular chest and the breadth of his shoulders. She couldn't ignore his goose bumps.

He was freezing, yet he hadn't reached for a share of the ample blanket. And if he'd intended to seduce her—she was hard-pressed to imagine any other reason that he'd climb into bed with her—he'd apparently abandoned his goal. As far as she could tell, he was honestly sleeping. With his eyes open.

It didn't make sense.

There were times, of course, when a woman didn't need the total picture to take appropriate action. "Get the hell out of my bed, Courtland," she said irritably.

Without hesitation—without any sudden speed, either—his hand lifted from her lap and shifted behind him for balance. He swung both long legs over the side of the bed and stood up. For the briefest moment his profile was silhouetted against the window light, and Bree felt an unwilling catch of emotion.

Her stereotype of a sleepwalker was someone who moved like a robot, arms outstretched ghost fashion. She guessed Simon was sleepwalking, but he was no robot . . . and he wasn't the formidably cold Mr. Courtland.

He was just a man—human, vulnerable—with the weight of trouble in his eyes and a silence about him that spoke to Bree of a terrible isolation and loneliness. His long, lean frame moved in the shadows as soundlessly and fluidly as a predator stalking the night . . . but Simon was no predator. Not tonight. When he walked through the doorway, his stride was aimless, blind. Lost.

She pictured him roaming the house for the rest of the night, half-naked and cold, and nearly ran after him.

For once in her life, though, she had the good sense to check her impulsiveness. Simon had made it clear he wanted nothing to do with her, and what could she accomplish? Her interfering would only embarrass him. His problems weren't hers. Tossing aside the blanket, she climbed out of bed, closed the door and this time firmly latched it.

Yet when she wrapped herself in the blanket again and tried to close her eyes, she kept seeing his. Lost and bleak. And how often did he spend the darkest hours of the night wandering alone? What was he looking for? What if he hurt himself? What kind of stress made a man sleepwalk, and surely there was someone in his life who could help him?

They were rhetorical questions. Fairly fascinating rhetorical questions, but she would never know the answers.

Impatiently she pushed herself into a sitting position against the couch back. In another hour or two, it would be light. She didn't have the stamina to face the road without a little more rest, but there was no chance of oversleeping if she dozed sitting up. It was suddenly important to her to obey Simon's mandate about being gone before he wakened.

Creaking, shadow-haunted old houses didn't scare her; she welcomed risk and had yet to find a challenge that threatened her.

Curiosity, though, was her oldest nemesis. Courtland wasn't her worry—she didn't even know him—but he uneasily reminded her of the nasty pattern of mistakes she'd worked so hard to break. She wasn't going looking for trouble, not again. In the past, when she saw someone hurting, she'd jumped in. She'd cared before, given before, committed her heart and soul—damn easily—before. And ended up battered every time.

A sleepy voice in her mind suggested that she was making a mountain out of a molehill. What was the big deal? One more hour's sleep, and then she'd be gone.

There was nothing to be afraid of.

TWO

Bree didn't budge for hours. She slept like the dead, but her dreams had been sabotaged by a rogue in navy boxers...a rogue with troubled, wounded eyes who chased her through the night, catching her once in a shadowy woods, another time in a dew-damp field under the brazen moonlight. Both times he'd stripped off her white linen shirt and taken her naked, ravaging her with merciless, shameless, passionate creativity. It was disgustingly corny stuff.

When Bree pried her eyes open, she balefully realized that the sun was dazzling high. There was only one thought in her groggy head.

She had to get out of here.

Faster than a speeding bullet, she made the bed back into a couch, neatly folded the blanket and peeled off Simon's shirt. Her red sweater, jeans and jean jacket had humorously dried in accordion pleats, conforming to the shape of the radiator, but they were toasty warm.

She grabbed her leather purse and tiptoed to the door, praying that her host was happily snoring on the second floor, because she was stuck infringing on his hospitality a little longer. She needed a bathroom. Her mouth was as dry as a cave and her face needed a good splash of cold water.

Silent as a thief, she unlatched the den door and whisked down the hall toward the kitchen wing. The house was different by daylight—less spooky and more like a charming white elephant begging care. Cruel sunshine illuminated cracked paint, scarred woodwork and musty dust. Cobwebs danced from the brass chandelier over the stairs. The sheet-covered furniture only made the house look lonelier, and not for the first time since she'd arrived, Bree wondered how on earth Simon had happened to be here.

Also not for the first time, she ruthlessly reminded herself that cats lost most of their lives due to curiosity.

She'd nearly reached the kitchen when she stopped dead, startled by the sound of a small crash, then the scrape of a pot, then the unmistakable sound of voices. Voices—as in two. Until that instant, it hadn't once occurred to Bree that there was another human being in the household.

One of the voices was a raspy, sexy bass, pedantic in tone; it wasn't hard to recognize. The other voice had a rasp, too, but it was a raspy soprano. A distinctly feminine soprano.

"After breakfast, we're going to call your mother."

"Yes, Daddy."

"You're going to apologize for giving her absolute hell."

"Yes, Daddy."

"You scared your mother half to death, and you're old enough to realize what you were doing, Jessica. It's not like there was any excuse. She adores the ground you walk on, and I think that's half the problem. Divorce is supposed to be hell on a kid, but that's where you've got her buffaloed. You've been taking advantage of the situation since you were three years old. And as far as this last hunger strike—"

The phrase "hunger strike" jarred Bree. She couldn't help peeking her nose around the corner. Initially she'd assumed from Simon's sonorous, reasoning tone that he was speaking to his daughter and that his daughter was the ballpark age of a teenager.

His daughter was ballpark four. A pudgy four, who was sitting squat on the kitchen table, listening gravely and intently to her father's lecture with her legs swinging. She had Simon's deep-set, quick gray eyes, but hers were magnified behind a tiny pair of blue-rimmed glasses, and she'd inherited her father's sandy-brown hair. Where his was styled Wall Street, though, hers was a snarled, springy tangle that fell to her shoulders. She was wearing orange tennies, no laces, paired with red jeans and a misbuttoned blouse. Unless Bree was mistaken, the small mouth was garishly painted with bright pink lipstick.

"The bottom line, Jessica, is that you're going back to your mother. You can't stay with me."

"Sure, I can," Jessica said patiently. "I'm here, aren't I?"

"I know you're here, but that doesn't mean you can stay."

"Sure, it does."

"No, it doesn't."

"Sure, it does."

"Jessica—"

"Who's she, Daddy?"

Bree hadn't meant to step in, but first the four-year-old had captured her attention and then the room did. Last night, the marvelous old-fashioned kitchen had been pristine neat and a cook's paradise in potential.

No more. Bowls and cracked eggshells and scattered dishes littered the counter. A congealing disaster on the stove might have been—an optimistic guess—a lumpy attempt at pancakes. Apparently when the pancakes failed, Simon had tried French toast. The sink reeked of burned, eggy bread, and there were pockets of dribbling puddles all over the floor.

It wasn't a little mess, it was a terrible mess, so terrible that Bree was tempted to laugh aloud. The impulse died when Simon's head whipped around to the open doorway.

Right off, she knew that her passionate snuggler had no knowledge of his nightly escapade. Just like a werewolf and a waning moon, daylight apparently obliterated any memory of weakness in Simon. He was back to being the *gros chien* she'd first met. His cords were creased, his white button-down fresh, his judgmental scowl intimidatingly in place.

He took in her rumpled clothes, unbrushed hair and bare feet at a glance. A speaking glance. He'd expected her to be gone. Bree could see that, but when she studied his face, she thought vaguely of escaped criminals. Desperate, haggard, driven. Shadows wreathed his eyes; his skin was white with fatigue. His shoulders were as wide as an ax handle, but he could carry another ten pounds and still be lean. Maybe he didn't eat, and how long had it been since he'd had a solid night's sleep? And the whole house, his daughter, the state of the kitchen . . . Bree felt a helpless stir of sympathy. Heaven knew how it had all happened, but it wasn't tough to guess that Simon wasn't the type to enjoy complications or messes. And he did seem to be over his head in both.

"Who's she, Daddy?" Jessica repeated.

"Ms. Reynaud was stranded in the storm last night."

"And I'm leaving," Bree assured him swiftly. "If it's all right with you, though, I'd like to use your—"

"Go ahead."

"I like the way you talk," Jessica informed her.

Bree couldn't resist a conspiratorial wink at the little one—from the one eye out of Simon's vision. "I like the way you talk, too, *chère*." A lingering conversation wasn't wise. She quickly tiptoed past that dark, disapproving gaze toward the bathroom.

"She talks *wonderfully,*" Jessica told her father.

"She talks differently," Simon immediately corrected her. "It's because she's from a different part of the country."

"Where?"

"Somewhere south. I don't know. It's none of our business, and you're not going to distract me, young lady. You and I—"

"I'm starving to death, Daddy."

Silence. "Didn't we have breakfast?" More silence. "God." A sigh louder than the north wind. "All right. There are two more boxes of groceries. Somehow we're going to find a way to produce something edible, and then I'm calling your mother."

"Yes, Daddy."

Bree didn't mean to eavesdrop—naturally, she'd closed the door—but it wasn't her fault the old-fashioned door had a transom. It was cocked open just enough that she could hear their voices—until she started running water. She washed her face, brushed her teeth and scrounged in her bag for a little make-up. The whole routine never took her five minutes, yet she found herself dawdling for ten.

"You see this one? It's loaded with natural vitamins and fiber. It'll make you grow big and strong and healthy. But this one is loaded with preservatives and nasty chemicals and sodium, and it has no natural food value whatsoever. It's completely up to you, Jessica. I'm not going to influence your choice in any way."

"Great. I want Captain Cracko."

A moment's pause. "Were you listening to me?"

"Yes, Daddy."

"You don't want Captain Cracko."

"You said I could choose. You promised."

"I didn't *promise,* and I assumed you would make the right choice."

"I made the right choice," Jessica said in the same patient, pedantic, reasoning tone she'd learned from the obvious source.

Bree found herself grinning, yet as she piled blush and lip gloss back in her purse, she was losing the smile. Simon seemed to be under the insane impression he could talk to a four-year-old as if she were a member of the board. It didn't say much for his knowledge of children. Truthfully, Bree couldn't fathom how he'd managed to conceive a child to begin with. It took more than getting naked to have sex; it took emotion. So far she hadn't seen Simon unbend enough to even smile.

Except, of course, last night. Around three in the morning, Simon had been very real. Very human. A defenseless man with sad gray eyes and apparently a need—a desperate need—to find someone to hold on to in the night.

Suddenly aware that she heard no more voices, Bree latched her purse and stepped out of the bathroom. The child had disappeared, although evidence of the argument's victor was on the table—a bowl heaped with Captain Cracko that was rapidly becoming soggy in milk.

Simon sat in the captain's chair at the head of the scarred oak table, looking totally thrown for a loop. His legs were sprawled and his eyes were closed. The instant he realized she was there, he snapped to a formal sitting posture and blessed her with one of his imminently dependable scowls.

"You're leaving now?" He didn't say "please, God," but it was in his tone.

"I'm more than willing to pay you for the night's lodging," she mentioned.

"Forget it."

"Actually, I feel a little uncomfortable with that." It wasn't true, even remotely true. There seemed to be an invisible little devil putting words in her mouth.

"The storm scared me, and you can't imagine how grateful I was for a roof over my head. If you won't take money, maybe there's something you'd let me do."

"I don't want payment and you don't need to do anything, Ms. Reynau—"

"Bree," she firmly corrected him. "And it wouldn't take me longer than a few minutes to clean up this kitchen."

"The offer is appreciated but unnecessary. I'm sure you want to be on your way, and I..." Briefly, unwillingly, his gaze lanced from disaster to disaster in the sunlit brick and French-blue kitchen. When he glanced back at her, she diagnosed all the symptoms of a defeated man. He wanted her gone. Badly. Just not quite so badly as he wanted to face that disaster of a kitchen alone.

"It's not your problem," he said flatly, but his tone was weaker.

"Of course it isn't, but it wasn't your problem when you took in a stranded traveler last night. Honestly, it wouldn't take me half an hour to make this livable again. Unless you have some objection...?"

She was pretty sure he had objections. Lots of them. But when he opened his mouth, they never got said.

Bree pushed up her sleeves.

The minx was still there at dinner, which totally confused Simon. He hadn't clawed his way to a six-figure income by being stupid about people, but he couldn't figure Bree for love or money.

She could have left at eleven that morning. Instead, out of the goodness of her heart, she'd stuck around through the day and taken on Jessica. At lunch, she'd produced an unlikely concoction with the name of dirty rice. Now it was six, and Simon warily lifted the fork to his mouth to taste another unfamiliar ethnic dish.

The flavor of sauce and spices immediately assaulted his taste buds. It wasn't good. It was mouth watering and delectable.

Ms. Reynaud was one tricky cookie, and he was beginning to find the situation as aggravating as a hangnail. Gourmet cooks didn't drop out of the sky, and neither did guardian angel baby-sitters. Bree had come from absolutely nowhere and, for no motivation he could fathom, worked like a dog all day. Somewhere there was a catch.

With a woman, there was always a catch.

"I love this stuff, Bree," Jessica piped in.

"It's excellent," Simon affirmed.

Dancing blue eyes drifted over his face. "Ah, *cher,* you sound so shocked. When you first saw the table, I could swear you looked as worried as a man risking poison."

Her drawl was as familiar and teasing as if she'd known him for years. That familiarity jarred Simon like the sharp scrape of chalk on a blackboard.

Across the table, he watched her lips close on a forkful of food and marveled. She even managed to eat provocatively, which was the more astounding because her figure could pass for a ten-year-old boy's. She wore no bra beneath her red sweater. She was as flat as a pancake. There was nothing keeping up her jeans except for a little twitch of hips, and Simon had never been aroused by a pair of long, skinny legs.

He ate more dinner and frowned. It wasn't the body that made a man feel restless and edgy. It was the way she moved, lithe and limber, and with that little swish in her behind. There was something immoral about that swish.

There was something dangerous about her altogether—a judgment that Simon sensed was unreasonable and unfair. Bree had disturbed him from the moment they met. He didn't like the way he reacted to her, but more to the point, he didn't understand it.

There was nothing in her face to make a man so wary. Her hair was a lustrous blue-black, worn straight, long and swinging down her back. The style couldn't be simpler. Her skin was fine pored and porcelain clear, her nose had just a little tip, her chin was neatly squared off. The composite was attractive, even striking, but hardly earthshaking. Her mouth—small, soft and evocatively red—definitely spelled trouble but Simon could hardly hang her because nature had endowed her lips with healthy color.

It had to be the eyes, he decided shrewdly. No good woman had eyes like that. Her brows had an irreverent arch, the lashes were darker and thicker than smoke, and the color was a startling bright blue, full of sparkle, full of sexy sass. And across the table, he saw her lips suddenly curl.

"I'm beginning to think I have a fly on my nose, Simon," she murmured. "If you have a question on your mind, I can't imagine why you haven't asked it."

"I don't have a question." He had a hundred.

"No? You were certainly frowning hard about something."

Well, hell. She'd opened the door. "I was just wondering..." He motioned to the rapidly disappearing food on the table. "When you offered to 'throw something together,' I didn't know you were going to come up with this. It's excellent. So excellent that you could probably make a living as a chef."

"Is that what you were wondering? How I make a living?" She blithely heaped more food onto her plate. As far as Simon could tell, her appetite rivaled an elephant's. "Actually, I don't worry too much about making a living. In fact, some people would probably classify my life-style as one step up from a vagrant's." She smiled.

He told himself that she deliberately smiled like that...and used words like "vagrant." As if she knew—which she couldn't—precisely what it took to get under his skin. "No interest in a career?"

"Oh, I had one of those for a while. I sat in a secretary's chair for several years, wooing profit and loss statements out of a computer terminal, mastering a mischievous copying machine, wading daily in the incomparable excitement of office politics."

"I take it business didn't hold your interest?"

"Couldn't stand it," she admitted cheerfully.

Maybe she'd guessed that his entire life was business. Maybe she hadn't. Either way, Simon knew it was wiser to shut up, but somehow he couldn't. "You're how old? Twenty-five?"

"Twenty-seven."

"You must have found something you want to stick with."

Her shoulders lifted in a negligent shrug. "For a while now I've fooled around with what you guessed—

cooking. It fit in well with a traveling life-style. Whether you're in a small town or a metropolis, someone's always short a cook, and it's been fun ... introducing southern Pennsylvania to cush-cush, Iowa to *couche couche, beignets* to Michigan.''

''What's *couche couche?*'' Jessica had been listening to the entire conversation.

''Something wonderfully good for breakfast,'' Bree told her, and would probably have gone on if Simon hadn't interrupted.

''So how long have you been having ... fun ... traveling across the country?''

''A little over a year.''

''Over a year,'' Simon echoed blandly. ''Just going anywhere and any place?''

''Yes.''

''No steady job, no career goal in mind?''

''Not a one.''

''Living out of a car, relatively hand-to-mouth? And alone?''

Bree cupped her chin in her palm. ''I think there's a chance that we're distantly related. At least, I've heard parts of this conversation before from some of my five thousand relatives.''

''I didn't mean to offend you,'' he said stiffly.

''You didn't offend me.'' Bree automatically saved his urchin's milk before the glass had a chance to spill. ''I have four older brothers who drill me with the same conversation every time we're on the phone. Their main concern, of course—being brothers—is that some guy'll assume I'm fast and loose because I'm a woman traveling alone. Not, for a minute, that I thought that idea crossed your mind, Simon.''

He was getting such a headache.

"I'm fast and loose," Jessica informed the table at large. "Nobody beats me when I'm running good. If you're not fast enough, Bree, I can help you."

"Thanks, love." But those deep sloe eyes were still fastened on his face. "As I've told my brothers more than once, I can take care of myself—a lesson I first picked up in the back seat of a Buick when I was sixteen. Regardless. A year ago I had a dream...to see the country, to find out how other people lived, to learn all I could before I was tied down and the chance was gone. Haven't you ever had a dream?"

Simon didn't respond. There was nothing he could say—not without coming across like a pompous jerk—and he figured he'd already done enough of that. Still, he didn't totally buy the idealistic dream business. Past the sassy pepper, past the free spirit rhetoric, there was something in her eyes—a woman's secrets, a woman's vulnerability. He found himself worrying about what had happened to her in the back seat of that Buick and decided he was losing his mind.

He had a dozen problems on his plate. None of them included a troubling stranger with big blue eyes.

When Bree started dishing up ice cream for Jessica, he excused himself, lurched out of his chair and strode for the telephone in the hall. For the tenth time that day, he dialed the Rapid City number for his ex-wife.

Liz had been in no mood to listen to him when she'd dropped Jessica on his doorstep the day before. Jess excelled in timely disappearing acts and sieges of muteness, but her latest prize trick was hunger strikes. It had broken Liz's lovingly maternal back.

Anyone could look at Jess and know she wasn't starving. He was sure she had somehow eaten on the sly. But when she wanted something, she was capable of putting Liz through hell until she got it. In this instance, what his daughter apparently wanted was time with him.

Simon would have walked on water if his four-year-old needed him, but that wasn't the case, and under the present circumstances there was just no way he could handle Jess. Liz hadn't realized. She'd been too upset to listen, but he knew his ex-wife. Whatever his personal feelings about her, Liz was a caring and devoted mother. She'd be missing Jess by now. She'd be calmed down. He'd be able to reason with her.

The phone rang a dozen times before Simon clapped down the receiver. It was tough to reason with a woman who wasn't home, and obviously he couldn't drive Jess back to Rapid City until he located Liz.

He swiped a hand over his face. His eyes burned, his nerves felt stretched to the point of snapping, and he was losing a vicious battle with a very bad headache. He hadn't slept well since he could remember.

He was old friends with stress, but not a battering case of exhaustion like this. His management consulting business demanded twenty-hour workdays, but he'd lost his chief engineer last month—doubling the work load at a time when three contracts were in the works. Then Uncle Fee died. Simon barely knew the eccentric old hermit—he'd never wanted to inherit this house and never expected to be made executor of his great-uncle's will. Still, there was no one else in the family to do it, so yesterday he'd packed up Jess, an overnight case and his computer equipment. So what if he missed a few more nights' sleep? It couldn't take forever to clear up his distant uncle's affairs, and the first step was obviously to see the place.

He wished he hadn't.

The house wasn't fit for rats, and this was ranch country. God knew where he was going to find a plumber, electrician and carpenter in the middle of nowhere. Simon doubted even God knew where he was going to find a buyer for the Gothic albatross once it was fixed. Adding to the mess were Uncle Fee's collections—artifacts, fossils, antiques. They were too valuable to leave in a deserted, unprotected house. A horde of distant relatives were avidly waiting to divide the take, but the collections had never been cataloged or appraised. Simon could do most of the research through the computer, but it was going to take time.

Reams of time.

Time he didn't have and couldn't afford.

Time that was enormously complicated by a four-year-old whom Simon loved more than life but couldn't conceivably caretake in a filthy old house where the heat was barely functional.

He already knew he would handle it all. He always did. He hadn't made a fortune by ducking from a challenge. His whole life he'd specialized in the un-solvable problems, the unwinnable battles. He'd yet to find a crisis he couldn't resolve with systematic organization, order and control.

He was just so . . . beat.

"Simon?"

He looked up. Bree was standing in the doorway of the shadowed hall, a dishcloth in her hands. In silhouette, her legs looked even longer and skinnier, two women could have fit in her sizable sweater, and her feet were bare. They'd been bare all day. She was apparently allergic to shoes, and he was apparently incapable of looking at her mouth without thinking of sex and sin. Simon had no time for sex and sin, and he simply couldn't fathom the aggravating attraction he felt for her.

Naturally, he could ignore the attraction, but he never ignored a moral debt. He hadn't asked her to stay... but she had, and Jessica had taken to her like a kindred spirit. If she hadn't stuck around, Simon was embarrassingly aware that he would probably still be in the kitchen, unraveling the mysteries of pancake batter.

"I just wanted to tell you that Jess is upstairs. I promised to read her a story, and then I'll be leaving."

"No, you won't."

"I beg your pardon?"

Simon sighed. He hadn't meant it to sound like an order. Maybe it was her eyes, maybe her mouth, maybe her damn bare feet, but he looked at her and something made his back bristle, his voice sound stiff. It was sheer idiocy, particularly when he'd known this issue was coming for hours. "If you leave now, you'll be driving in the dark," he said more reasonably.

"I've driven in the dark before."

"You don't know the country. I do. You're not going to find any place closer to stay than Rapid City."

"I'm not too tired to drive," she assured him. "It's not a problem."

It was for Simon. She'd been stranded last night with a stranger. God knew she'd been safe with him, but some men would take a look at those sultry blue eyes and long legs and give her a hard time. Simon had seen her car. In this part of the country, potholes were bigger than Volkswagens, and he was going to seriously lose his mind if he didn't get some rest soon. He wasn't going to get any rest if he was worried all night about her getting stranded again.

He tried a backdoor approach to the subject. "My daughter took to you like a duck to water."

She leaned a shoulder in the doorway and smiled. "She's a love."

"We must be talking about two different children. My ex-wife can't even keep a baby-sitter without offering combat pay."

Her smile broadened. "You're never going to have to worry about her bending in the wind. Something tells me it's an inherited characteristic."

The comment startled him. "We're nothing alike."

"No?"

"Are you joking? She runs circles around me. I never know what I'm supposed to say to a four-year-old with eye shadow plastered over her eyes." Simon caught himself dragging a hand through his hair and straightened. "The issue is that you gave up your day for my daughter," he said impatiently. "You probably didn't realize that I was in a bind—"

"Oh, I realized it." She folded the dish towel in her hands. "Jess chatters like a magpie. It wasn't hard to pick up that her mom left her yesterday—not expectedly. And that she thinks the sun rises and sets with you."

She didn't need to say that she didn't share his daughter's opinion.

"The relevance is that I had a hundred things to do that would have been impossible if you hadn't been here for Jessica. I don't know what motivated you to stay and I don't care. As far as I'm concerned, I owe you a night's lodging, and you can't seriously want to head out on unfamiliar roads at this hour."

Her soft eyes swept over him, studying, thoughtful. "My reasons for staying the day were uncomplicated. My time is free, I liked your daughter, and I wanted to. None of that puts you under any obligation."

"I'm aware of that, but—"

"You don't want me to stay another night, *cher*."

She said it gently, not like a challenge, yet her perception provoked him. Simon was not an open book. She was never supposed to realize how uneasy she made him feel. "That isn't true," he said testily. "I wouldn't have made the offer if I didn't mean it."

She hesitated, this time long and seriously. "You're going to worry if I'm on the road, aren't you?"

"No."

Again a smile, fainter than a whisper. "I think you would, and I have to confess that you confuse me, Simon. You're still not absolutely positive whether I'm going to steal the family silver, yet you're going to feel guilty if you throw me out on the road this late at night."

She was beginning to exhaust him. The buttery magnolia drawl was sinfully misleading. She was sharper than a tack. "I never thought you were a thief."

"Perhaps not in the usual way. I'd guess that you trust very few people with your daughter, yet you trusted me with Jessica...so maybe it's just on another level with you and me that there's a problem? You wouldn't—by any chance—be a teensy bit worried that I'm going to sneak upstairs and seduce you in the middle of the night?"

He pinched the spare flesh at the bridge of his nose. He handled four-million-dollar contracts. People worldwide treated him with respect...occasionally to the point of annoyance. He'd built a business from nothing, took care of more parasitical family members than he cared to count and had never owed anyone anything—a principal that made for neat, clean relationships over which he had total control.

Why was it that every encounter with this one small woman made his control feel shot to hell? "Ms. Reynaud," he said wearily, "I'm thirty-five years old, and until tonight, have never had a problem having a rational conversation with a woman."

"I just wanted you to know you were safe."

Three

———

CHAMEAU. Bree snapped the key in the lock to the den door, then dragged over a straight chair to hook under the doorknob. If Simon chose to sleepwalk tonight, it wasn't going to be near her. *Chameau refoule.*

She frowned as she turned to the couch. She was way out of practice if "a repressed cow" was the most colorful insult she could think of for Mr. Courtland. No one could beat a Cajun for colorful insults.

She pulled out the bed, then laid out the sleeping bag she'd brought from her car trunk. After that annoying conversation with Simon, her intent had been to hightail it down the road, but that was temper talking, not good sense. As he'd said, it was late, and she had no idea where she was going to end up the next day. Spending one more night gave her the chance to wash her hair and rinse out a few clothes, and heaven knew she was beat.

She tugged on a yellow nightshirt, jerked off the light and settled in. In the pitch dark, though, she seemed more in a mood to fume than sleep. Good grief, she'd been *joking* when she asked if he was afraid of her seducing him in the night.

Well. She hadn't exactly been joking. More like testing the waters to see if a little sexual innuendo might raise a spark in Simon. If it had, she'd be on the road right now.

It hadn't. She clearly had as much sexual appeal to Simon as a rabid dog.

And that was a relief, Bree judiciously told herself. She definitely felt safer about spending another night, but talk about your ice-veined, buttoned-down, stiff-necked Mr. Pompous! *Nothing* could make that man crack a smile, and he was hurtfully judgmental for someone who didn't know her from Adam.

Absolutely the only reason she'd stayed the day was because of Jessica, poor baby.

Bree's eyes blinked open in the darkness. To be truthful, Jessica was no one's poor baby; she was a four-year-old little rascal. They'd had a wonderful day. Bree had always been a sucker for a child, and Jess had more uninhibited creative energy than any ten adults. Bree's only uneasy moments in the entire day were when the urchin had brought up her father.

"Daddy needs me," Jessica had explained to her that morning. "Mommy has lots of people to take care of her, but Daddy has no one. Except me."

The scamp adored her dad. Bree couldn't fathom why. All day long Simon had sat in front of a computer keyboard, punching buttons. Punching buttons was probably the nearest he ever came to sexual pleasure. Nothing else seemed to stir him to life.

Bree had watched him all day. It wasn't that he didn't notice his child or care. He made a point of giving Jessica time; he loved his daughter and it showed, but holy spit! Simon talked to the kid as if she were ninety years old. Jessica didn't give a hoot about "quality time." She wanted to roughhouse. She needed a cuddle.

As far as Bree could tell, Simon was in an emotional vacuum. He simply had no concept of life, enjoyment, laughter... and the look of him in the hall that evening had badly upset her.

For a few seconds, he obviously hadn't realized she was standing there. His hand was still on the telephone, his head leaned back against a stuccoed wall. He wasn't just tired; he was weaving from exhaustion. His eyes had been glazed; she'd guessed he was fighting a migraine, and two seconds after he'd put Jessica to bed, the stupid jerk had headed right back to his office for more work.

Not, Bree thought firmly, that she'd chosen to spend the night to make sure Simon was all right.

She'd opted to spend the day because of Jessica. And she'd opted to spend the night because it was a practical decision.

The months on the road really had changed her. Finally, she'd gotten smart and developed some judgment. Far too many times she'd become involved in a relationship solely because someone needed her. Simon didn't need her. Simon couldn't even stand her.

And the feeling was mutual. Sleepily, Bree resolved to be gone by daybreak . . . and absently remembered another Cajun phrase. *Je l'emmends.* It meant 'to hell with him' and rather precisely seemed to summarize her feelings about Simon. She fell asleep on that musical litany. *Je l'emmends. Je l'emmends. Je . . .*

The stroke on her cheek was as soft as a stroke on her soul. Her lashes fluttered, opening and closing, her vision blurred between a dream and reality. Somewhere, a French door gaped open, letting in a draft of spring night air and the silvery illumination of a full moon. It was a wonderfully romantic view to wake up to. All Bree could think of was *not again*.

The door to the den was still locked, the chair still neatly propped against the jamb so no one could get in. From the hall.

She had never once considered that a sleepwalker would climb in past the brambly weeds on the terrace and through the outside doors. Much less naked. Or nearly naked. Simon was wearing black briefs tonight. He'd also unzipped her sleeping bag.

Bree closed her eyes and mentally considered strangling him. The night before, his sleepwalking had been a source of both fascination and honest concern. That was before she knew him. He was an arrogant, cold, unlikable son of a sea dog. Maybe he walked in his sleep because he had some deep, dark, traumatic and pitiful problem, but she no longer cared.

A thumb gently brushed her cheek again. Reverently. Tenderly. It took a moment before she oriented herself. Simon was lying on his side, facing her. Like the night before, his eyes were open.

A man half-conscious should have a vacant stare. His eyes were as dark as the devil-rogue's in her dreams, just as lustrous, just as hungry. A shiver chased down her spine from nowhere. Come on, Reynaud. This isn't real. This isn't dangerous. He doesn't have the least idea what he's doing.

His thumb traced the fragile line of her cheekbone. The warmth of his palm cupped her hair. He leaned up—she hoped he was getting up to leave—but then his head bent over hers, shadowing all light. His lips touched down, playful, alluring, whisper soft.

It wasn't a long kiss. She caught the faint taste of cognac, the texture of his sleep warmed lips, the scent of his skin. The kiss was more promise than substance. A gift, not a demand. And nothing, suddenly, was so simple for Bree.

He lifted his head, looked at her and then settled back against the pillow. Her breath was incomprehensibly thready. She'd been kissed before. Plenty of times. She was stupid about men. Had *always* been stupid about men, and was even more stupid about love. She'd never managed the sensible business of loving halfway. Never managed to see, in time, that any man was willing to take advantage of a sucker.

Only there was nothing aggressive or selfish in Simon's touch. His palm slid down her long white neck and lingered there. His thumb gently soothed the throbbing pulse beat in her throat. Slowly, softly, he stroked the curve of her shoulder, dipped under the sleeping bag and caressed the length of her side. And he looked at her.

She kept trying to tell herself that it was Simon... but she knew deep down it wasn't. Her midnight caller was warm and sensual and terrifyingly perceptive. If he'd just grabbed her, she could have slapped him. He didn't grab. He didn't take. He simply caressed her skin with gentle, tender, infinite allure.

She was sleepy. It was dark. She'd been alone for a year of nights, and alone in a soul sense her whole life. "Simon..." she said desperately, and only won herself another kiss.

This time his tongue was involved. Wet velvet. Soft. Coaxing her closed lips to open, not forcing them, and when they did, that soft, soft tongue was a gentle invasion. He discovered the smooth finish of her teeth. He discovered her tongue, hiding in the roof of her mouth, not wanting to be found. He found it.

She trembled. "Dammit, Simon—"

He lifted his head and smiled, then took her mouth again. Dominantly. Completely. She could feel the heat and power build in his body, heard the drag of his breath, and heat coiled inside her as sure as fire.

He kissed her again, an aggressive promise of pleasure, an intimate wooing. His warm palm dropped to her collarbone, then her breast. It was as if he knew...that she could be painfully sensitive. Few men had bothered to discover that small size concentrated sensation, not diminished it. She was still wearing the bright yellow cotton nightshirt. She seemed to swell to a 40 D under the insistent, erotic, sensual rub of his thumb.

And if her imagination was running to that size, she knew she was in serious trouble.

Her voice was hoarse and wobbly. "Go back to bed, Simon."

He stopped the delightful rubbing.

She took a breath, searching for strength that wasn't there, needing common sense when she felt as fragile as rose petals. "Simon. I want you to go. Directly out the door. Upstairs. Back to your own bed."

There was no change in mood, no difference in the way he looked at her by moonlight. But he obeyed. She felt one last soft stroke on her cheek, then the lifting of weight from the mattress. As slow as a stalking cat, he walked toward the door.

She blinked, then vaulted out of bed. Scurrying ahead of him, she lifted the chair, flicked the lock and jerked open the door.

Just in time for him to walk through.

"Hi."

Bree opened her eyes to a glare of sunlight, noted dismally that she'd once again missed daybreak by several hours, and groggily squinted at her visitor. Jessica was sitting cross-legged at the foot of the bed, picking at a tiny scab on her knee. Her attire for the day was apparently fluorescent orange underpants, three crunched-down pairs of socks and one of her father's white oxford cloth shirts.

"Wanna make some cookies?" the child asked hopefully.

Bree shook her head. "Can't. We talked about it, remember? I have to leave this morning." Her head was still muzzy, her limbs heavier than lead. Had she slept at all after Simon left? Her gaze wandered from the locked French doors at the terrace to the den door, which was standing ajar, when it couldn't be. "Honey, how did you get in here?"

Jessica matter-of-factly stuck her hand in her shirt pocket. She held up a long brass key, then repocketed it.

"Does your daddy know you have that?" Bree asked suspiciously.

"Daddy knows everything," Jessica informed her, then pushed her blue-rimmed glasses further back on her nose and returned to the subject that mattered to her. "I'm gonna die if you don't stay."

Bree climbed over the covers and wrapped her arms around the little heart tugger. "We had a good time yesterday, didn't we?"

Jessica's mournful eyes followed her as she bounded out of bed and pulled on white jeans, a belt and a khaki shirt. A few seconds with a brush and her hair was pleated in a loose braid. A few seconds after that she was folding up the sleeping bag and ignoring the growl of her empty stomach with the same determination that she ignored the child's mournful eyes.

Two nights with a sleepwalker was enough. As soon as she got away from Simon—a fast five hundred miles away from Simon—she was bound to see the humor in the situation. For months she'd successfully locked up her emotions. Yet during the span of two nights, a man she barely knew had turned the darkness into magic, made her hotter than butter spitting in a skillet and touched her, inside and out. She'd been so sure a man like that didn't exist—a warm, caring man with a giving heart, a man who made her feel protected, cherished. In the most impossible of all places, she'd found him.

There were just a couple of teensy flies in the ointment.

Simon didn't have any idea what he'd done.

And Bree could barely stand the man by light of day.

Get the lead out of your fanny, Reynaud. You're bumping this pop stand before you get in more trouble than you already are. Yet she had to stall leaving for a few more minutes. Dropping her sleeping bag and tote, she hunched by her woebegone friend with the shimmering eyes. "I need a smile before I go, *chère,* and this is no morning to be sad. I know we had fun yesterday, but you don't need me to be busy today. By now I'm sure your dad has reached your mother—"

"It doesn't matter if he talks to Mom. I'm staying with my dad."

"I know you think that." Bree smoothed the wild tendrils of hair that had sneaked from the child's ponytail. Yesterday, one of the reasons she'd been determined to stick around was to make sure the four-year-old was really, honestly, totally okay. No, it was none of her business, but Simon seemed uniquely inept at parenting, and what kind of mother deserted her kid? At first glance, it had been easy for Bree to make some worrisome assumptions about both parents.

Her assumptions had been wrong. She still didn't know the mother's story, and Simon's handling of his daughter made Bree shake her head, but she'd unquestionably spent the day with a healthy, creative, uninhibitedly affectionate child. Jessica was full of the precocious devil. She was also secure, the way only a child who'd been raised with love and caring could be. "You told me a little about your mom yesterday," she said. "Sure sounded to me like you love her to bits."

"I do."

"And I'll bet she's missing you."

"I miss her, too, but I'm staying with my dad. And I've thought it all out. I can take care of him myself, but it'd be lots, lots easier if you stayed around, too. Sometimes he's a little hard to take care of for just one person."

Bree personally thought it would take a legion to take on Simon, but refrained from mentioning it to his ardent lobbyist. "I have to go, Love. I'm sorry."

"Please, Bree? *Please?*"

The hound dog eyes had absolutely no effect on Bree. Thank heavens she had developed more fortitude than she used to have! She blithely tiptoed past the closed door to Simon's office and took a fast five minutes in the bathroom. Without a qualm, she strode past the unique chimney oven she'd never have the chance to try, the mysterious, sheet-draped rooms she'd never have the chance to explore.

Once outside, she sucked in an invigorating gulp of the spring-fresh air, patted the head of one of the snarling stone lions and then busily stashed her clothes and sleeping bag in her VW's miniature trunk. Simon's somber Mercedes was parked farther up the driveway, close to the three paint-peeling barns that had snagged her curiosity yesterday, but Bree kept her attention pinned west.

She'd driven out of the Badlands the night of the storm, but in the distance she could still see the needlelike spires and colored, streaked hills that had first captured her fascination. There were some forty thousand acres in the national park just begging to be explored. The sun was dazzling bright, the morning spanking brisk and breezy. It was a wonderful day for a footloose, heart-free roamer. The possibilities were limitless! She could go anywhere! Do anything!

Cut the nonsense, Reynaud, she told herself. You're so miserable you're ready to cry. You couldn't possibly have become attached to those two Courtlands this quickly. Now move it out. She rested a last lingering glance on the dreadfully ill-conceived castle in its setting of tumbleweeds and range grass, shook her head and climbed into the car. She was just strapping in when the front door banged open.

"Is she with you?"

"Jessica?" She told herself it was a relief to see him, because she immediately felt better about leaving. He'd dressed real wild this morning—his button-down was oxford blue instead of white—and the authoritative growl in his voice was exhaustingly familiar.

He took the steps down to her car two at a time. "Of course I mean Jessica, unless you know of any other four-year-old terrorists on the property. She's not with you?"

"No."

"Then have you seen her?"

"Not in the last fifteen minutes, but she can't be far." In spite of herself, her gaze rested on his face. The first time he hadn't remembered his nocturnal adventures, but this morning she'd been so positive he would. How could a man kiss with that much sexual dynamite and not *know?* "Are you sure she isn't in the house?"

"I've been calling her blue for the last five minutes."

"Well, she didn't use the front door if she walked outside, because I would have seen—"

"This has to be your fault."

"My fault?" Bree, bristling, unsnapped the seat belt and jerked open the car door. The wind brushed a streak of color on her cheeks as she faced him, hands on hips. Irritation made her heart slam, not their sudden closeness. She'd take cyanide before admitting an attraction to Simon . . . at least the daytime Simon. "I don't know what you think is my fault, but you're obviously overreacting. I just *saw* the child. Just because she didn't jump for your dictatorial bellow is no reason to think she's lost."

He didn't deny the dictatorial bellow. "I didn't say she was lost."

"Well, then—"

"She's missing, not lost. Jessica has a habit of hiding out when she doesn't get her own way." Simon's eyes narrowed on her face. "You must have said something to her."

"I certainly did not. I . . ." Bree swallowed, suddenly remembering how determined Jessica had been for her to stay.

Simon rolled his eyes skyward. "I *knew* it was linked to you." With one hand rubbing the back of his neck, his gaze swiveled around the yard—and lighted on the barns.

Bree had only stolen a peek yesterday, enough to realize the buildings were packed with probably a century of falling down debris. It wasn't a safe place for a child. "She wouldn't go in the barns," she said swiftly.

"She'd go anywhere she thought would scare us the most," Simon grimly corrected her. Then he was gone, jogging through the weeds toward the deserted back buildings.

Bree hesitated all of two seconds, then pelted behind him, with him and then past him. "I'll take the far one."

They checked all three buildings and found dust, junk and filth in abundance—but no four-year-old. More by accident than intent, they ended up sprinting back toward the house at the same time. Arguing.

"This is not your problem."

"You made it my problem when you accused me of being responsible."

"You are responsible for making her think you're the hottest thing since a cat's meow. She wanted you to stay, didn't she? That's what this is about?"

"You're making it sound like she wanted to keep a snake in her room."

"I never said that."

"You were thinking it."

"I wasn't. I was thinking that I was going to kill her when I find her."

"Simon—" He was barreling through the front doorway when she caught his sleeve. "I don't know why I rub you wrong, and I don't care. But don't be harsh with her, all right? She's still half a baby."

He stopped dead and stared at her in complete confusion. In those few seconds before he closed the door, sun streamed in, catching his wind-ruffled hair and the intense fire of emotion in his eyes. His shirt was untucked, his chin scraped with a smudge of dirt, and Bree felt her pulse skitter with awareness. He wasn't the self-contained and controlled Courtland at that moment, but as real and human as the sleepwalker who'd so dangerously disturbed her nights.

"Have I been harsh with you?" he demanded. The thought seemed to astonish him.

"Come on, Simon. You took a dislike to me on sight—"

"That isn't true. At least my behavior toward you had nothing to do with . . . dislike. You were stuck for two nights with a man you barely knew. It was perfectly logical to me that you would worry about being . . . safe. You could have misinterpreted friendliness. You could have thought I wanted to come on to you. You could have . . ." Abruptly he slammed the door with a scowl. He quickly changed the subject. "You thought I'd hurt Jessica? Are you nuts? I've never laid a hand on that child in her entire life. She's my *daughter!*"

That seemed to sum up the subject to Simon. It summed up a completely different subject for Bree. Later, she would mull how hard he'd worked to deny any "inappropriate" feelings for her, but right then his emotion for his daughter mattered more. She'd so wrongly thought him pedantic and cold when his capacity for love was fierce, powerful, huge. His child had been misplaced for all of twenty minutes. He was ready to batter down steel walls, leap buildings, tackle tall bears.

"Why," Simon said wearily, "are you smiling, Ms. Reynaud?"

"Bree," she automatically corrected him.

"I don't see anything funny in this situation."

"Come on, Simon, she's a fan of mischief, not danger. If you'll just calm down and stop wringing your hands, you'll realize there's no reason to be so upset. Jess has a terrific set of vocal chords. If she'd even stubbed her toe, I'm sure you'd have heard them. Neither of us has absolutely any reason to think she's hurt."

"No?"

Good heavens, the sky was going to fall. He was actually listening to her. "No," she said reassuringly.

Yet it took another hour of searching before a whim of Bree's paid off. The dining room had already been scoured a half-dozen times before she suddenly thought to lift the door of the old-fashioned dumb-waiter. When she saw the tip of an orange tennis shoe, she felt her stomach drop. Heaven knew how old the ropes on the pulley system were—certainly old enough to be rotten or weak.

Simon jerked up the door the rest of the way, quickly revealing a bare knee, then a wrinkled shirt, then the beginnings of an irrepressible grin. Finally Jessica ducked her head out. Her eyes were as bright as Fourth of July sparklers.

Simon lifted her to the floor, his hands lingering on her shoulders. "Jessica, you must never do that again."

"Yes, Daddy."

Bree's palm suddenly itched.

"You're old enough to understand irresponsibility. Hiding out is no way to effectively solve any problem. There are places all over this house and land that are less than safe for a child. I want your promise that you'll ask me before going exploring again.''

''Yes, Daddy.''

Bree's palm itched harder.

''You're capable of using judgment. I know you can comprehend that there are times you simply can't have your own way. Next time, I want you to try and think a problem completely through—''

''Yes, Daddy.'' The little one's eyes pounced on Bree's. ''You're here. I knew you would be. I *knew* I could make you stay.''

''Did you, *chère?*'' Bree didn't mean to bump Simon's hip, but she needed to get closer to Jessica— close enough to bend the child over one arm and raise her other arm for ballast.

''Bree!''

She heard Simon's shocked voice just before her palm connected, solidly, with the four-year-old's fanny. The child's responsive howl must have echoed through three floors. Bree spun her around and faced her nose-to-nose. ''If you *ever* pull a trick like that again, your daddy'll give you six of those and an hour in your room. Got it?''

''Yes, Bree.''

''You scared your dad half to death. Say you're sorry. Right now!''

''I'm sorry, Daddy.''

Bree gently wiped a streak of dirt from the child's cheek, her tone softening. ''Okay, we're square. It's all forgotten now—except that I think your dad needs a kiss. And then you might want to scoot up to your room and change that filthy shirt.''

Jessica threw herself into her father's arms and shortly thereafter threw herself up the stairs with equally abandoned zest. In the sun-dusted dining room, there was abrupt silence. Complete silence. There was a glint of something in Simon's eyes, but Bree couldn't read it for love or money.

"You spanked my kid."

"One quick swat is hardly a spanking. Did you see any tears in her eyes? Even one?"

"I didn't say you hurt her—"

"I'd walk on nails before hurting a child. Any child. And that goes a million times over as far as Jessica."

"A swat is still a swat."

Bree winced guiltily. "I know." She hugged her arms around her chest. "If you want an apology, you have one. I was dead wrong to interfere and I feel terrible. Worse than terrible. I feel like slime—but for cripe's sakes, Simon, can't you remember being a little kid and having done something wrong and just wanting it over with? I just couldn't stand there and watch you mete out the inhuman punishment of talking her to death."

Another glint. This one evocatively delivered beneath hooded lashes, and his tone came out measured. "I was trying to reason with her."

"That pulley system has to be older than the hills. If she'd sneaked in the dumb waiter when it was on the second floor, she could have been hurt. You don't reason with a child under those circumstances, Simon. You do something, immediately and fast, to make absolutely sure she never does it again." Bree warmed up to the subject. She didn't claim to have a parent's experience, but she definitely had some first-hand memories of what worked with an incorrigibly reckless free spirit. Heaven knew, she'd been one. He could ask her father if he didn't believe her....

"Oh, I believe you. In fact, I have no problem at all believing you were a perfect little hellion," Simon said blandly. "Bree, would you stay?"

She heard him. She was simply positive she'd heard wrong. "I beg your pardon?"

"Would you consider staying?" Simon repeated.

Her lips curled in an immediately sympathetic smile. "It's okay. I guessed that you've been under an incredible amount of stress," she said gently. "We all say things we don't mean when we're feeling a lot of pressure. Try a hot cup of tea, *cher*. You're bound to feel more like yourself—"

"I asked you to stay, Bree, and I can assure you that I'm in my right mind and that I meant it."

Four

———

"She confounds me."

"Come on, Simon. She's your own daughter." Bree fished around in the bottom of her purse and came up with a chocolate-coated breakfast bar. She bit off a good-size chunk.

Simon had dragged her into his office, asking that she at least hear him out. Bree was willing to listen; she wasn't willing to hear. Her old-fashioned Keds were making fast tracks for the nearest exit as soon as he finished his spiel, but she had been curious why he always locked his office.

Now she knew. Like the rest of the house, the room was bulging with a hodgepodge of weirdly shaped objects covered in dust sheets, but Simon had cleared out a working corner for his electronic sanctuary. Computer, modem, fax, printer, backup power system—

Bree figured that Jessica could destroy the whole setup in five seconds flat. If she were Simon, she wouldn't screw around with locks. She'd put up barricades.

"Look, I'm not asking you to stay forever. Just a few days. Until I've located my ex-wife. That can't possibly mean more time than a long weekend. Liz has never left Jessica before without giving me a phone number or address where I could reach her."

"Simon..."

"Just listen, all right? I'm a management consultant—engineering. The business requires a lot of short-term, quick trip travel, but I can do the real core of the work anywhere that has a computer and fax—it wouldn't matter if I lived in a cave. That has to be one of the reasons Fee chose me to be executor of his will. Apparently he thought I was more flexible than the other family members."

"Fee?" She peeled down the wrapper for the last half of the chocolate bar. Personally she thought that anyone who considered Simon "flexible" needed analysis.

"My great-uncle. The last time I saw him, I was five. He holed up here most of his life and pretended the family didn't exist. I never saw this house—which for some horrific reason seems to be mine—or the house's contents, which aren't, making them a different kind of nightmare."

"Simon..." He was definitely digressing.

"The house isn't in shape for a dog to live in, much less a child. The plumbing's nip and tuck. The heat's hit-or-miss. I could keep Jess fed if there were a microwave—there isn't—and there're a hundred things she can't touch. For one small example..." He lunged out of his desk chair and lifted the dust sheet just behind her.

A sliver of chocolate almost stuck in her throat. Apparently she'd been sitting right next to a three-foot-long skeleton with a headful of carnivorous teeth.

"Ye old Mesohippus from the Oligocene epoch. In more recent times known as a three-toed horse," Simon said wearily. "Fee kept quite a zoo of dinosaurs. They're all over the house. You take off a sheet, thinking you're going to find your basic chair, your basic floor lamp, and instead there's a bunch of bones staring at you."

He threw himself back in the chair. "It's too far for me to commute from my apartment in Sioux Falls, and I can't just walk off and leave it. I'm responsible for the disposition of this stuff—some of it is worth a fortune—but I can't do a thing until it's all been cataloged. In the meantime, I have a living to make, a four-million-dollar contract on the line—" he flicked his computer screen as if to illustrate "—I'm supporting a mother, an ex-wife and a younger sister who couldn't cut it financially after a divorce. They all think money grows on trees. I'm damn good at making money, but I have no idea what I'm supposed to do with a four-year-old who specializes in terrorism. For God's sake, can't you stay a few days?"

Bree couldn't help but smile. Simon was playing this up like a criminal's last appeal—he wasn't really that desperate—but she had to confess to feeling charmed. Beneath the poker-faced expression was a definite personality. She'd never guessed he had a wry, dry sense of humor. Even more, she'd never imagined that he would unbend enough to have a natural conversation with her. Heavens, he was actually relating. "I understand that you're feeling a little under the gun, *cher,* but—"

"A thousand bucks. Three days."

Her smile died. "That's bananas!"

"A thousand five. Dammit, I've never seen her take to anyone the way she takes to you, and the feeling is obviously mutual. I've seen the way you are with her—"

"Courtland, would you kindly button it for a full five seconds and relax?" Bree threw her legs over the sides of the cavernous wing chair. She'd finished her breakfast bar and it had failed her. She'd counted on the chocolate to give her a jolt of caffeine. She needed a jolt of strength from somewhere, because, Lord forgive her, she seemed to be weakening.

It was easy to chuckle at the picture of the compulsively orderly and organized Simon wandering through a house full of fossils. It wasn't so funny, now that she understood the weight of responsibilities he carried. And there was nothing remotely humorous about a man already over his head with pressures suddenly saddled with an urchin who had no concept of the term *peace and quiet.*

Both printer and fax machine were spewing paper onto the floor. Simon paid them no more attention than she did. Although he methodically rolled up his shirtsleeves, his eyes never left her face. He'd been patient a full minute—probably a record—yet Bree found herself at a loss for a sure decision. She was pitifully susceptible to people who needed her—always had been, always would be. It would be easy

enough to stay for a few days if the only issue was
Jessica.

She wasn't afraid of Simon, she told herself. Rather,
he *upset* her. Simon wasn't all pompous starch. Throw
him out in some sunshine, mess up his Ivy League
haircut, paste a smile on his face, and he'd be a helluva hunk. Bree had never been attracted to hunks, but
she wondered what it would take to make him laugh.
She wondered how long he'd been driving himself so
hard. She wondered if he even knew that he was
lonely.

"Look, Bree—"

She swiftly interrupted him. "How did you sleep
last night?"

"Sleep? What does that have to do with—"

"I know the question sounds silly, but humor me,"
she coaxed.

"I slept fine," he said impatiently.

She looked. There was no flicker in his beautiful
dark eyes, no pulse suddenly jumping in his throat, no
change of expression in that dominantly male bone
structure. Without a lie detector test, she couldn't be
absolutely sure of the truth...but she was. Simon
could be a royal pain, but he wasn't a liar. He'd probably die before yielding an ounce of that unbudgeable
integrity, which left her with the same old conclusion.
He honestly had no idea what he did in the middle of
the night.

He must have sensed her weakening, because his
gaze abruptly narrowed on her face. "Two thousand—"

"Oh, for cripe's sake." Bree dusted the crumbs
from her lap and stood up. "If you bring up money

one more time, I'll walk out this door so fast it'll make your head spin.'' She could taste the flavor of a bad mistake, yet out it came. "I'd be perfectly happy—delighted—to stay with Jess for a couple of days, Simon. Assuming we can come to terms."

"Fine."

"You haven't heard the terms," she reminded him, and began. "No money."

"No money? You have to need money—"

"You mention money again and the deal's off. And *I* cook. Not you. You stay away from my kitchen."

"I think," he said dryly, "that I could manage that."

Bree continued to tick off conditions on her fingertips. "You have no caffeine after six at night. You don't work after dinner. Before going to bed, you have a double cognac—"

"I beg your pardon?"

"Don't bother begging my pardon, Simon. Those are my terms."

"But those terms don't make sense."

"Take it or leave it, but I want your word if you agree."

"Reynaud, you're talking about sipping some fool cognac when I just offered you two thousand dollars—"

She whipped around and headed for the door. Simon muttered a pithy swearword and jerked out of his chair. He beat her to the doorway by a hair, but then he just stood there with a perplexed frown. "I don't understand you," he said irritably, yet abruptly he shot out his hand.

Some contracts were considered legally binding with a handshake. Bree felt more as if she were making a deal with the devil. His hand was big, warm and hard. Whether or not Simon knew it, the last time she'd made contact with those big, warm hands had been in bed. And she'd felt a butter-melting sizzle of pure female sensuality that had embarrassingly shaken her.

She'd excused her idiotic responsiveness to him on the obvious grounds. Both times, she'd been wakened from a sound sleep. The middle of the night was a time of fantasies and dreams. The sleepwalking Simon had reached one of her more inane fantasies—the dream that she would find a man, the one man who would take the wealth of love she needed to give without using her. The dream, like all dreams, was unrealistic. Yet on those nocturnal sojourns, Simon hadn't hurt or threatened her in any way.

She felt threatened now. No one raised in the heat and humidity and jungle greens of a southern Louisiana bayou could be insensitive to omens. The hand shake was short—Simon certainly drew back fast—but the effect was there. A pot of emotions suddenly heated to simmering. Sunlight suddenly turned up to higher wattage. The rest of the room faded like an old blurred snapshot, because her awareness of Simon as a man was suddenly that sharpened.

Cripes, Reynaud, get a grip. This is no dream lover. Maybe you have some reason to be wary of Hyde, but this is Jekyll. This is Simon. This is real life.

And abruptly she relaxed. Simon needed a little help. It was going to be fun giving him help on her terms. It couldn't be that hard to find a place to sleep that had a dead bolt, and hell's bells, she'd only committed to staying a couple of days.

* * *

"Simon?"

He heard the familiar feminine drawl. He just ignored it. For five hours straight he'd been glued to the computer screen. His computer was connected to a data base covering the Oligocene and Pleistocene geological epochs. Truthfully he didn't give a hoot about either, but he'd found a couple of collectors interested in his great-uncle's fossils. It went against his grain to be cheated, which meant that before he flew either of them in, he intended to know more than they did.

"Mr. Courtland."

Eyes stinging, back aching, nerves yapping from sitting in one position too long, he swung around. "What?"

"We would appreciate your company for high tea."

"For what?"

"For high tea, Daddy."

The two visions in front of him curtsied. The shorter one was swathed in lace, a boa scarf, orange tennis shoes and a handmade paper fan. Her hair was swept up in a French twist suited to a thirty-year-old.

The older vision was wearing a floor-length gown in funereal-black lace. Either the dress was built strangely, or Bree had miraculously gained thirty pounds—tufted pounds—on her behind since breakfast. A white pearl comb held back her hair, and somewhere she'd come up with black button shoes of ancient vintage.

"This—" Bree gravely pointed to her sidekick "—is the queen of England, I'm the duchess of Pookenanney, and we are currently serving high tea in the parlor."

Simon pinched his nose and closed his eyes. "Am I supposed to take this seriously?"

"You can do anything you like, as long as you move your *petit cul mignon, cher.*"

Simon may not know French, but he had a pretty good idea when someone was telling him to move his butt. He rose to his feet and briefly met Bree's eyes. During the past three days he'd entertained more than one fantasy about what he'd like to do with the woman if he caught her alone for a fast five minutes.

He had a killing work schedule ahead of him, but he trailed her ridiculously bobbing bustle into the "parlor." Ms. Reynaud undoubtedly believed she'd finally whipped him into a docile-dog state.

She was dead wrong.

Grave as a judge, his gaze strayed the length of the long, old-fashioned living room. She'd done it. Hauled open the drapes, stripped off the dust sheets, vacuumed and dusted and waxed and fussed until everything was to her liking. This wasn't the only room she'd taken on. She'd never asked permission. He never wanted or expected her to work like a dog, and he'd never met a nosier woman in his entire life.

Bree had one speed. Fast. And she did everything the same way—exuberantly, impulsively, passionately. The house was one thing, but where she really snagged his sense of humor was when she attempted to take over his life. "Get reckless, *cher.* Wear a sweatshirt," she'd say. Or, "Poor baby, did you really think the whole world runs like a game of Simon Says?" She mandated a daily hour of exercise, sergeanted balanced meals, and as regular as a clock, a

vase-size glass of cognac was placed in front of him
around nine every night.

And she was obsessed with that cognac. He
generally drank the equivalent of a snifter and si-
phoned the rest back into the bottle when she wasn't
looking. If it was any other woman, Simon might en-
tertain the interesting notion that she wanted him
drunk . . . but he never had been and never would be
that much of a fool.

She didn't like him. She didn't say that she thought
he was an arrogant, repressed, compulsive workaholic, but there was a hot-fuse charge whenever they
were in the same room. It wasn't hard to snag her
temper—not that she ever blew up. She just started
muttering a lot of French words under her breath.

Simon himself had no temper. He had too much
control.

And rather than strangle her, he generally bent to
her rules—not because he'd miraculously turned into
a malleable, obedient dog—but because Bree was like
a dangerous breath of fresh air. His family had always resented his taking charge. Employees generally
kowtowed to his authority. Liz used to say that he'd
lost his humanity—she was probably right—but nobody had had the nerve to challenge him in a long
time.

Just Bree.

Generally, tongue in cheek, he'd simply been playing along with her bossy ways—but this afternoon was
different. The day before she'd caught him on the raw.
The little witch was teasing him. She obviously took
joy—*great* joy—in teasing him, but she'd made some

coaxing comment about his not knowing how to play with his own child.

It hurt then.

It still did.

So much so that if the four-year-old in the boa scarf wanted him to attend a tea party, he was damn well going to attend a tea party. And to behave with appropriate decorum for the situation.

"Have a seat, Sir Simon."

The duchess and queen flounced down on the Victorian brocade sofa, but for a moment he nearly panicked. He couldn't find their "high tea." Abruptly he noticed the doll's set of tiny dishes on the lacquered Chinese coffee table. His thumbnail was probably bigger than one of the cups. "Sugar or lemon, sir?" Bree asked crisply.

"Pardon?" He was wary of doing the wrong thing. He didn't care if Bree swore at him in French until the next blue moon, but he wanted his daughter happy.

"Do you want sugar or lemon?" Jessica echoed.

"Sugar," he murmured carefully.

The two sat with spines straight as dowagers. The queen of England poured. The duchess delivered a sugar cube to his cup. Only there wasn't any tea and there wasn't any sugar.

"You aren't drinking, Daddy."

"Oh." Following their lead, he lifted the thimble-size cup to his lips. Noting Bree's behavior, he stuck out his little finger. Both of them were holding their cups with their little fingers stuck out. They sipped.

"Would you care for a cucumber sandwich?"

"Yes, Sir Simon, would you care for a cucumber sandwich?"

There weren't any of those, either. Take it seriously, Courtland, he reminded himself, but that was increasingly hard. The two of them were acting nuttier than fruitcakes. He couldn't remember the last time work pressures and responsibilities hadn't dominated his mind. That wasn't a choice. It was the way real life had stacked up from the time he was fourteen. Survival was a war. You were never so stupid as to let down your guard—not when you had other people to take care of.

Only he found his mouth starting to twitch when the duchess, after the third imaginary cup of tea, so gravely leaned forward and placed her slim hand on his knee.

"You can't leave quite yet. We have a little entertainment planned for you," the duchess murmured. He'd never seen a woman with sassier eyes in his entire life. "The queen would like you to hear a little musical rendition that she's prepared especially for you."

"Musical?" Jess couldn't sing "Happy Birthday" on key.

"She has entitled this particular requiem, 'Ode to a Crow.'"

"And you're gonna love it, Daddy."

An old upright stood in the far corner. His daughter threw her boa scarf over a shoulder, seated herself on the piano stool with a flourish and promptly attacked the yellowed ivory keys. The sound that emerged when the untuned piano was coupled with his daughter's untutored skill threatened true deafness.

Flats crashed with sharps. Keys banged together in screaming disharmony. If Simon were a dog, he would have howled.

Eventually—none too soon—Jess tired of her unforgettable requiem, stopped playing and looked up. The duchess sprang to her feet, loudly applauding. "Bravo! Bravo!"

Simon also sprang to his feet but apparently not fast enough, because he felt the sharp jab of an elbow in his ribs.

"Throw roses," the duchess whispered.

"Throw . . . ?"

"Roses." She was wildly strewing thin air.

He just couldn't take it. He'd tried. It was a helluva thing to hang over a father, that he could be neglecting his daughter by not playing with her, and he'd done his absolute best to be a proper knight or an earl or a sir—or whatever had been in Jess's wild imagination.

But he just couldn't help it. He covered his face but the first chuckle escaped. An irrepressible laugh followed the chuckle, and in a moment he was laughing so hard that he had to hold on to something.

And there was Bree.

Simon's laughter had sounded *wonderful*.

Bree couldn't stop thinking about it. Carrying her shoes, she sneaked up the stairs to the third floor. The hour was midnight, the whole house dark. Quiet as a cat, she closed and locked the door to the tiny attic room before switching on the overhead light.

She simply couldn't believe how laughter had transformed Simon. His shoulders had loosened up.

His face had lost its harsh austerity, the look of rigid control. His eyes had come to life with a dangerously sexy sparkle, and there'd been a brief moment when he'd clutched her shoulder. Her head had reared back. So had his. He'd looked at her mouth....

Impatiently Bree stripped off her orange T-shirt and her jeans. It didn't matter how he'd looked at her mouth. It mattered that Simon could be coaxed away from incessant work, coaxed into joining real life again, coaxed into expressing natural feelings—at least toward Jessica.

Stark naked, she crossed the room to the far wall of floor-to-ceiling cupboards. She'd discovered the castle's strange "tower" room three days ago, and it had immediately intrigued her. No curtains softened the casement windows, no carpet warmed the cold floor, and there wasn't a stick of furniture in a house that was stuffed to the gills everywhere else. Out of curiosity, she'd started pulling the knobs and handles on the wall of cupboards.

One massive "drawer," to her surprise, had yielded a pull-out double bed, Murphy style. Another had pulled out to reveal a bedside table, with lamp. The house's architect had had quite an eccentric sense of humor, but right then and there Bree had known where she was going to sleep.

Before coming upstairs each night, however, she carefully closed the den door and made sure the sleeper couch was pulled out. It just seemed wiser to let Simon believe she was still sleeping there. Either her little trick worked or the exercise and healthy diet she'd forced on him were working some natural magic of their own. No midnight visitors had disturbed her rest for three nights now.

That was a good thing, because by bedtime she was inevitably as whipped as a tired puppy. Yawning, she pulled out the bed. Jessica was a trip. She had a wild imagination, an indomitable spirit and was as stubborn as a goat. Jess reminded Bree far too much of herself as a kid. Vaguely she told herself to send her mother a dozen roses daily for the rest of her life, and Lord, her dad... Unfortunately the only way she could make it up to her dad for being such a terrible child was by giving him a grandchild. Raoul was counting on one who was twice as much trouble.

She flipped off the overhead light, and in the darkness crossed to the north window. The latch made a creaking noise if she wasn't careful. She was careful. It was windy tonight, windy and wild. The brace of fresh air immediately feathered over her bare skin, raising gooseflesh and pumping up her blood when all she wanted to do was sleep.

It seemed the height of irony that she'd solved the problem of Simon's nights only to develop a sleep disorder of her own. Restless energy plagued her the moment the lights were out.

The days were worse. Jessica was game for anything as long as it was active. They'd roamed the hills and done plenty of playing, but Bree had also cooked up a storm and made an adventure out of cleaning up the old house. Hunger was a terrible thing. She hadn't known how much she'd missed a home. Any home. Not a motel, not a temporarily rented room, but the kind of place where children made horrific messes and baking smells invaded the kitchen and the windows had a shine because you put it there.

She'd missed it.

The security and familiarity, even the housework, and definitely the company of children. She had dozens of nieces and nephews and cousins. She'd always wanted a child. Moonlight burned on her suddenly closed eyes. All right. She'd always wanted a half dozen.

Life, of course, didn't always work out that easily.

Shivering hard now, she closed the window and climbed into bed. The sheets were freezing, but she huddled, knees to her chin, and gradually warmed up. She thought about families and children; she thought about homes and security and Jessica. She thought about the windswept canyons of the Badlands and the history of the land the Sioux had called "Maco Sica."

And when she was tired enough, she let herself think, just a little, about Simon again.

With a little teasing, a little bullying, he was already acting better toward Jess. Drag the man away from work; henpeck him into some decent food, rest, exercise, and good grief, he was . . . almost human. As far as she could tell, Simon had simply gotten lost somewhere in that vast land of "supposed to's," where the responsibilities of his life ruled him instead of the other way around.

And Bree was deliriously happy that she wasn't involved. How many times had she responded to a lost soul and given everything she had? And then been taken, roughshod, flat, with her heart in the ante and no aces in sight.

Luckily there was no risk of that with Simon. They had as much in common as a lark and an owl, and they both knew it. He treated her more warily than barbed wire. He never touched her, never tried. Except for a nightly chess game—which she'd initiated to get him away from working every evening—he generally avoided being in the same room with her.

Bree felt safe with Simon, more safe than she'd felt around any man for years. It was a wonderful, luxurious, deliciously secure feeling.

She heard the quiet unlatching of the door around two.

Five

─────

At first Bree thought she imagined the click of a key in the lock. She sensed no movement, heard no other sound. A heavy bank of clouds blocked any hope of moonlight. The room was so dark that she couldn't see anything but layers of shadows, and Lord, she was tired. She'd been tossing and turning for more than an hour now, dark thoughts chasing her every time she closed her eyes. She assured herself again that the sound of the key was just her imagination. After all, how could Simon have found her?

But he had. One of the shadows was moving. She caught a wink of light—the window reflection off his sandy hair—and before she could open her mouth, his hip depressed the mattress near her side.

She was tempted to bay like a depressed hound. The first time had been intriguing, the second disturbing,

and a third time—if she had any say in the matter—
was not going to happen.

"Go back to bed, Simon."

He'd obeyed the other times. Immediately. This
time he leaned closer. As though he could see in the
dark, his palms slid onto her scalp. Long, cool fingers caught, then sieved through her tousled hair. His
thumbs pressed gently where her temples were hot with
headache, throbbing from sleep that wouldn't come.

It felt good. So wonderfully good that for a quick,
quick second she almost gave in to the cosseting magic
in his fingers and closed her eyes. Almost.

"Look, *cher,* this is *loufoque, zinzin, maboul.* Or
in any language on earth, bonkers. Now stand up, go
out the door and walk back downstairs to your own
bed."

Specific instructions had been helpful before. Tonight, they were worth a wooden nickel. Like the
stroke of a spring breeze, his forefinger brushed her
lips, silencing her. His fingers combed back in her hair
and began massaging her scalp. He rubbed and
kneaded, his movement all somnolent and slow and
soothing.

Bree told herself to wake him. Technically the
problem had never been more complicated than shak-
ing him awake, but she was afraid of making that
choice. For one thing, there was that old folklore
superstition of never waking a sleepwalker. Maybe it
was silly, but what it if were true? What if she caused
him some deep, dire, terrible trauma by waking him?

And there was a second, more worrisome reason she
hadn't made that choice. Even the first night, she
hadn't been afraid of the sleepwalking Simon; he'd

troubled her, yes, but he was so uniquely defenseless, so gentle, so oddly vulnerable. It had been impossible for her to believe he meant her harm.

It wasn't as if she thought a wide-awake Courtland meant her harm, either...but she just wasn't sure how he'd react to finding himself in her bed in the middle of the night, and no clothes in sight.

She clutched the sheet in a fist over her breasts, which protected her from precisely nothing. Tonight, he wasn't interested in breasts. When he finished the scalp massage, his entire concentration focused on collarbones and shoulders. He squeezed, kneaded, worked the taut muscles in her right shoulder, then her left.

She searched his shadowed face, studying hard, helpless to comprehend some *reason* why he was doing this. Was he dreaming? Was that what this sleepwalking business was about—acting out some dream? Some need? Maybe the only time he could let down his defenses was in the dark.

If that were true, she was having the same problem. She could feel the power in his hands, see the liquid warmth in his eyes, sense how close she was to his bare, warm chest. An inexcusable frisson of sexual awareness scooted through her bloodstream. No lover had made her feel this unbearably intimate. No man had ever made her feel this . . . tense.

"How about," she said desperately, "if I walk you back to bed? Would you like that? Could you try to remember that this is *me,* Simon? On a scale of one to ten, I don't think I'm even on your list. We get within two feet of each other and both of us start bristling like wet cats—"

Another brush of her lips. This time the edge of his thumb pleated the ridge of her lower lip, then traced the edge of her upper one. It was a lover's touch. Erotic, sensual and quite explicit. He wanted her to shut up.

Bree closed her eyes, praying for a miraculous answer to present itself. Simon simply resumed rubbing. Her upper arms, then her lower arms, then her hands. She'd never had a hand rub. He stroked her palm, gently pulled at her fingers, rotated her wrist. He wouldn't stop, and he made her hands feel... heavy. Before he was done, he'd made her entire body feel languorous, golden. It never occurred to her that she wasn't still clutching the sheet.

When he finished, his hips shifted higher on the mattress until his back was braced against the headboard. Before she could guess his intention, his hands snaked under her arms to lift her. For bare seconds, naked seconds, his fingertips pressed the sides of her breasts, but that contact was accidental.

He cradled her cheek to his chest. He tucked her arm around his ribs. And then he pulled, adjusted and cuddled the sheet and comforter close to her throat.

She waited the tick of a heartbeat, but that was apparently all he had in mind. No kisses, no embraces. Just drive a woman out of her mind, make her feel cosseted and cherished, turn her on until she felt pure liquid female... and then go to sleep. Sitting up. Holding her.

Bree jerked forward. Gently but firmly, his arm tightened. She lifted her head. His palm splayed in her spill of hair and pushed her back to his chest. No sucker in this life, Bree raised a knee. He made a

sound—the first sound she'd heard him make as a
sleepwalker—a low, throaty, whispery chuckle. There
wasn't much she could do with a knee tangled in covers.

"Dammit, Simon. You can't do this to me!"

His lips pressed on the crown of her head, soothing, comforting. Yet he wouldn't let her go. It was a
wretched sensation. It was as though he knew she were
troubled, knew that loneliness had been beating at her
like a hammer tonight, knew that she'd been tossing
and turning because too many empty, lonely nights
had gotten to her.

Simon couldn't know any of those things.

He *didn't* know any of those things. Yet he stayed.
And he held her. His chest hair tickled under her
cheek. His heart made a rhythmic da-dum, da-dum
right under her ear. And in time, because she couldn't
help herself, she dozed.

At six o'clock in the morning, the other side of the
bed was empty. Nothing stirred in the house, not even
dust, and the air was snuggling cold. It was an ideal
time to catch up on sleep, and Bree hadn't had a solid
night's rest since arriving in the Badlands. She told
herself to stop being an idiot and close her eyes, yet she
couldn't. She was too busy gnawing on a thumbnail
and glaring at the dots in the ceiling.

You've gotten to me, Courtland, and I don't like it,
she told herself.

Obviously lying in bed was getting her nowhere.
Grumpy, crabby, edgy, she crawled out of bed and
snatched up her jeans and a long-sleeved T-shirt. She
stumbled barefoot down both flights of stairs with

one, and only one, goal in her mind. Any man or beast who dared interfere with her direct route to the coffee was going to see some real violence.

Unfortunately, she was halfway through the doorway before she realized that the kitchen was already occupied.

Simon hadn't put on a light. The room was no brighter than a fuzzy, dawn-lit gray, but she could see he hadn't anticipated company any more than she had. He hadn't brushed his hair yet. He'd pulled on corduroy jeans but no shoes, no shirt, and his chin had a bristly stubble. He looked like a man who'd just climbed out of a woman's bed after a long night of hot sex.

Recently he *had* crawled out of a woman's bed, Bree thought irritably. Hers. Only he hadn't seduced her; he'd given her a hand rub, and she could not begin to fathom what had driven him to seek her out in the middle of the night. Companionship? But Simon was good-looking, smart and rich. He could have imported women in droves if he wanted some company. Nice women. Nice, formal, female executive types who talked in lectures the way he did—not Cajun Gypsies—yet Bree couldn't shake the stupid instinctive feeling that he needed her. Or someone. So badly that a soul-deep loneliness haunted his nights.

She had a rotten habit of falling for men who needed her, but at least all of them had been conscious. This was ridiculous. Packing her bags was the only solution, yet she was abruptly distracted from that train of thought. Simon was holding an old-fashioned coffeepot in his right hand and a measuring scoop in the other.

He hadn't realized she was there until she firmly whisked both out of his hands. There was no question that she was dealing with the formidable Mr. Courtland instead of her warm-blooded night caller. His shoulders defensively stiffened. Dark, dark eyes, dazed with exhaustion, immediately sparked to life. "I'm perfectly capable of making coffee."

"I know you are. I've tasted your brew, *cher*. You may want hair growing on your chest, but I don't."

Heavens. He cracked a smile. He probably didn't know that even the slightest smile transformed him from cold fish to hunk, and Bree certainly didn't care.

"You want some help?"

Help? If Simon had wanted to help her, he should have slammed the door in her face and left her to the mercies of a lightning storm a week ago. Furthermore, he was hovering. She really didn't need a close-up view of that bare chest. She'd already lain against that sleek, supple wall in the night, been tickled by those blond hairs, knew the smell of his warm, sleepy flesh. Mortifyingly, guiltily, embarrassingly well.

"I need to talk to you," she announced flatly.

"Before coffee?" His tone was appalled.

She couldn't argue with that. At that moment, she'd have killed for caffeine. It seemed to take forever for the coffee to brew.

They both stood at the window, watching the dawn shoot soft, pastel spears of color on the horizon. He didn't look at her, didn't talk, but he expelled a huge yawn that had him blinking in surprise.

Bree didn't smile, but most unwillingly, she could feel her sour-pickle mood shifting. The yawn made him sound so human, and she couldn't deny that the silence between them was oddly companionable.

When the pot finished perking, both responded like addicts for a fix. Simon pulled down two mugs. She poured. Simultaneously they took a mainline gulp of the rich, dark brew, swallowed and willingly burned their tongues for a second sip. Their eyes met in mutual lustful appreciation of the brew. Bree's immediately moved away. The lust in his gaze was real, but she was startlingly aware it wasn't all for the coffee.

It was bad enough being attracted to a phantom lover, but the last she knew, Courtland couldn't stand her. So much for the companionable silence. "I have to leave, Simon. As soon as possible, and preferably today. You *must* have located Jessica's mother by now?"

"I did. She's in Oregon."

"Oregon?"

"Oregon." Simon dropped into the captain's chair at the head of the table. "Liz called yesterday. It seems she's rented a vacation cottage on the coast. Rustic. No phone on the premises—"

The details were hardly relevant to Bree. She sank into a chair and drew up her knees. "But what about Jessica!"

"According to Liz, our daughter belongs with me. Not forever but definitely for now." His gaze drifted over her silky curtain of hair, her small red mouth, as though he were waking up on the look of her. Quickly he reached for his mug again. "It's not like I haven't always spent time with Jess, but it's usually short spurts—organized days, planned weekends. Liz claims, though, that the disappearing acts, the hunger strikes, all of Jessica's worst antics are over the issue of being with me. Ergo, she thinks it's best for Jess to be here. She said we'll talk in three weeks."

"Three weeks?" Bree's voice came out a squeak. "If you knew this yesterday, why didn't you tell me?"

"I would have—" he shot her a dry look over the rim of his coffee "—but then we had a tea party. I saw the way you played with my daughter. I saw the way I don't and have never known how to play with her. And I thought I might convince you to stay a little longer."

The old thumbscrew treatment, Bree thought dismally. He wasn't going to beg. He wasn't going to remind her that the house was about to be filled with plumbers and electricians and museum collectors interested in dinosaurs, and heaven knew how he would cope with Jess.

He was just going to look at her with those beautiful, dark, exhausted eyes.

Simon needed help. With his daughter, with this wonderful old house, and though he might not know it, with his nights. Never mind what bed he slept in; Bree worried about him at another level entirely. Left alone, anything could happen. What if he fell down a flight of stairs? Wandered outside and woke up completely lost?

Note that he's happily survived without you for years, Reynaud. You're not getting any further involved, and that's that.

Yet it moved her that he'd bucked his pride by asking her to stay. During the daylight hours they managed to coexist when the subject was Jessica. Simon didn't seem to worry that she was going to "contaminate'' his daughter, but Bree was pretty sure he privately saw her as an irresponsible rolling stone, probably as loose as a goose and twice as flighty. And to be truthful, she knew she'd done everything short of dancing naked on tabletops to encourage his attitude.

Hells bells, a woman couldn't always be nice, and he was so damned much fun to tease.

Irritably she plunked an elbow on her bent knee. No man was worth all this aggravation. The problem wasn't half as complicated as the solution. Courtland didn't really need her; he certainly didn't want her, and only one person was going to get hurt if she became more involved. It wasn't him. She had sworn a year ago to never again leap into a one-sided relationship. Who needed the grief?

"We could call it a job," he suggested.

"I don't want or need a job."

"I'm more than willing to pay you—"

"Oh, forget your stupid money, Simon. I told you before I don't want it," she said crossly.

He gave her one of those looks as if he wanted to check her eyes with a flashlight for dilated pupils. Simon apparently surrounded himself with people who motivated easily with a checkbook. Bree considered herself plenty greedy, but her real needs had nothing to do with money—a concept that Courtland would never comprehend. She waggled her bare toes over the edge of the chair, wishing she didn't feel tied up in knots. "Tell me something about your ex-wife."

"My ex-wife? What on earth does Liz have to do with your staying?"

"I didn't say she had to do with my staying. I just think..." One of these days she was going to put a muzzle on her impulsive tongue. "I just think that it's... unusual... how you talk about her."

"Unusual? How?"

"Because you sound friendly. Because you obviously respect her judgment about Jess. If there's any tension between the two of you, your daughter certainly hasn't picked it up. Most divorced people talk about their ex-spouses like the battle scars are still fresh. Not," Bree said swiftly, "that it's any of my business."

Simon raised his eyebrows. "You've never let that stop you before."

"Pardon?"

"I'm sure there are other people as curious as you are. I just haven't met any this side of Saint Louis. Regardless... in this case, you're hardly prying into any locked closet. Liz and I had a friendly marriage and an even friendlier divorce. End of story."

He was learning how to tease, she thought darkly. The one thing she'd taught him, and he turned it against her. An interest in people was not the same thing as nosiness. She could drop a subject faster than the snap of her fingers. Sometimes. "Come on, Courtland. If you got along that well, you'd still be married."

For a brief moment his eyes measured hers, thoughtful, considering. "What you and I consider a marriage, Bree, are likely to be two different things. I met Liz when she had just lost both parents in a car accident. It was a hard time for her... and I was there. For a while that was how the marriage worked—she was at a time in her life when she needed security, stability, protection. There simply came a point, as the saying goes, when she outgrew me."

He recited it like a lecture—facts, no emotion—and he continued on the same way. "We stuck it out an extra year for Jessica, but that was foolishness. Liz wanted out, and I knew it, and at the end we were living a cold war—that was no good for Jess. I don't know how other people handle a divorce, but from where I'm sitting, there is no excuse—ever—for any scenario where a child is caught in the middle. I don't agree with my ex-wife about a lot of things—she's overemotional, she overreacts, she lets Jess bamboozle her. But she adores Jess, so I keep my mouth shut and try to support her whenever I can. Now, is there anything else you want to know?"

Bree understood that he wanted the subject dropped, but she felt as if she'd walked into the last scene of a movie and missed all the critical parts. Had he married Liz because he wanted to or because she needed him? Hadn't he felt kicked in the teeth when his ex-wife wanted out? Did he realize how rare it was to hear a man willing to make any sacrifice to avoid putting his child in the middle?

She told herself to let it go, but one last minuscule question slipped past the gate. "Did you love her?"

His response was square, straight and as flat as a mantra's monotone. "Care for, yes. Love, no."

"Ever?"

"No." His eyes were chilled now. "As Liz would be the first to tell you, I'm not a passionate man. Or an emotional one. Now have you run out of questions, Reynaud?"

His gaze never faltered. Bree expected he intimidated whole boardrooms with those hard eyes and that quellingly sardonic tone. She wasn't intimidated, but she suddenly guessed why he was willing to share this little sidetrack conversation. He was warning her off: *This is who I am. Mr. Unemotional And Cold. Not a man who can keep a woman happy—even in bed.*

Bree had privately called Simon a lot of nasty names, but this was the first time she'd had reason to doubt his basic intelligence. Sure, she'd labeled him a cold fish on sight. She couldn't deny that he didn't do real well with expressing feelings.

But the lover in Simon broke out at night. Her midnight caller had passion to give and emotion to spare. He never took advantage, but on each occasion he'd perceived her needs and then responded with sensitivity and compelling tenderness. He made a woman feel safe...as if he knew what to do to take care of her. And he made a woman feel dangerous...because the hunger in Simon was so real—a huge, bold, masculine hunger to reach out, to touch, to hold. To love.

How could the idiot possibly think he was cold? Bree was tempted to shiver all over even imagining how he'd be if he was really awake and let loose in bed.

And as quickly as that shameless thought surfaced, she looked down to the last dregs of coffee in her mug. Something was wrong, because the distinction was blurring between the daytime Simon and the nighttime Simon. Either way she was reminded of a wild beehive she'd once found in the woods as a child. The lure of that potential rich, sweet honey had been her downfall, and predictably, she'd ended up being stung. Badly.

"You never said," Simon mentioned, "why you needed to leave so quickly."

"I just do."

"You're sure of that."

"Very sure." She sprang out of the chair, needing movement, action. His coffee mug was empty, so she fetched the pot.

"Somehow I had the feeling that you liked being around here." His eyes lowered to her neck, lingering on the bare stretch of throat above her loose T-shirt. "I just noticed that you're not wearing that necklace you usually do." He watched her overpour his mug with coffee, mutter something in French and then mop the spill with a dishcloth. "Jessica told me about it. She said it was a talisman, that you called it something like a *meron.*"

"Maron," she automatically corrected him.

"Maron, then." His tongue carefully rolled around the correct pronunciation. "You told Jess some folklore tale about these little seeds that float in the water on the bayous. She said the word *maron* means lost. That the Cajuns believe there's a lost soul living in the seed, so the superstitious carry a maron. It's their way of making sure a lost soul always gets home. You're not the least superstitious, are you, Bree?"

"For heaven's sake, we're headed for the twenty-first century. Of course I'm not superstitious," she said irritably.

"Hmm." His lips blew at the fresh mug of hot coffee. Then he took a sip. "Still, the necklace seems a curious talisman for a woman who doesn't have a home or even want one. It seemed possible that you might like to take root for a short time. Use an opportunity to take stock. Catch up on rest, rethink what you want. Not that I'm not sure you're perfectly happy living out of a car...."

If he took another potshot at her life-style, Bree was probably going to strangle him. More relevant, she was suddenly itchy and restless. Simon hadn't made his hoards of money being stupid. He wasn't good around people, but that didn't mean he lacked perception. He'd guessed she wanted some time; he'd guessed she was hungry for a home. He'd even guessed she was embarrassingly susceptible to a little omen here and there.

He knew enough about her to make her sincerely afraid. She already cared too much, already knew that a bookmaker wouldn't take odds on a relationship with Simon.

Courtland was a complex man with some obviously deep-seated emotions wandering around his formidable unconscious. Formidable, though, didn't always mean big. Bree kept having the sneaky feeling that an awful lot of ducks would line neatly in a row if he just had the right woman to keep him occupied—and very tired—in bed. Simon wouldn't have time to sleepwalk if he was busy. It wouldn't take much for the right woman to put him in touch with his feelings because, good grief, the passion was only a spare layer under the surface.

The *right woman,* of course, was the operative phrase. Bree knew she wasn't. He was an executive *gros chien.* And she was a Gypsy with ample experience in heartache.

Leaving was the only sensible choice, she decided, and turned around to firmly tell him that when she spotted Jessica in the doorway.

The child had scraped her tangled hair back with a tortoiseshell comb. Her shirt was red, her jeans orange. Floppy yellow socks completed her outfit, but not her makeup. Beneath the blue-rimmed glasses were eyelids lavishly adorned with green eye shadow, and somewhere she'd come across a pair of clip-on dangling earrings—old rhinestones—uniquely suited to a streetwalker.

"Hi, Daddy. Hi, Bree. What's for breakfast?"

The look of the urchin automatically made Bree chuckle, but her father didn't have the same reaction. The makeup, the earrings, the color scheme—Simon looked his daughter up and down and then lanced a frantic look at Bree. Gone was the businessman's authority, the aura of hard, cold-blooded control. Rhinestone earrings apparently didn't register in Simon's computer mind as reasonable. His gaze was desperate. It said, What am I supposed to do? For Pete's sake, help me.

Bree felt an imaginary chafing on her wrists as if someone had just tied her hands with emotional handcuffs.

She was definitely leaving.

Soon.

But maybe not quite yet. Simon loved Jess. He felt responsible for her. Conceivably he'd even die for the four-year-old hellion... but apparently nobody had ever told the big lug that he had the obvious and simple right to *enjoy* his daughter.

Six

There was an intricate engineering design on the computer screen—a layout for a mechanized warehouse system. Even before bidding on this Boston contract, Simon knew the system. He'd installed it in three other companies, but this time one of their engineering boys wanted a design modification. The idea was good, but it upped the overall cost by seventy thousand dollars.

Simon had never settled for less than the best before, and he didn't intend to now. Using the computer's graphics, he tried alternatives and then mathematically tested them to incorporate the modification—cheaply. Nothing worked. There were answers; it was simply a matter of finding them before next Tuesday. He wasn't the only engineering consultant bidding on this contract.

Even more than he wanted the contract, he wanted it done right, but the concentration had been impossible this past week. In a distant room, ladders scraped across wooden floors. Hammers incessantly pounded through the house. Voices carried, so did bootsteps, and so did the sudden bright voice at his side.

"Bree says to tell you to shut off the computer, Daddy."

"Can't now, sweetheart," he muttered. A multi-million-dollar contract, and he was stuck in a land of coyotes and prairie dogs.

"She says you have to. She says the guy has to cut the juice."

"Cut the...juice?" Jessica's usual reference to juice meant the apple and orange variety. It took him a second to realize that Bree had given his daughter an uncomplicated way to communicate that the electricity was being cut off.

Rapidly he saved the material and then exited. He flicked off the power. Behind him, sticky fingers latched around his neck in an affectionate stranglehold.

"Hey," he growled. That earned him a kiss on the cheek. A jam-sticky kiss. Before Bree had come along, his daughter had had no concept of order and control. Now she had less.

There was no breaking the urchin's death grip on his neck until he trailed a finger down her pudgy set of ribs. Jessica broke away giggling...a sound that had a curiously soothing effect on his frazzled nerves.

He gave in to a rare impulse and swooped his daughter high in his arms. Jess's response was more giggles, and Simon grudgingly heard Bree's Louisiana drawl in the back of his mind. *Forget the order and control. She wants to be tickled. She wants to be held. She wants you to roll on the floor with her.*

Assuming he was going to listen to advice—which he never did well—he wasn't likely to trust the judgment of an unemployed blue-eyed vagabond. Where his daughter was concerned, however, Bree had the nasty habit of being right. The weight in his arms, the smell, the textures of the mysterious four-year-old human being with the jam on her chin—it was hard to imagine anything that felt this good.

Always before, Simon had maintained a careful reserve with his daughter. He'd thought he had to. Jess was a precious and terrifying responsibility. Liz couldn't define discipline even with the help of a dictionary, so he assumed his daughter needed that from him. Even more, he wasn't good at getting emotionally close to people. Hell, he was rotten at it, and from the day she was born he'd felt inadequate about being a good father. *She's a kid, you idiot,* Bree kept telling him. *Just a kid. Love her to bits. This is complicated?*

"Where we goin'?"

"To the nearest sink to get your hands and face washed."

"Can't," Jessica said gravely.

"I promise you we can."

"Can't, Daddy. Really. There's no water."

He paused midstride in the kitchen. No water, no electricity, some thirty men running around creating noise and debris all over the house—if he had another week like this one, he'd go out of his mind.

He set Jess on the counter with her legs dangling and reached for a box of napkins. The crew's progress pleased him. Within another week it would all be done: new roof, new wiring, new furnace, insulation and the whole inside patched and painted. The mess was horrendous, but it was faster and more efficient to get it all done at once than to drag it out.

Technically, everything was going fine, but there were a couple of unexpected glitches that he hadn't anticipated. One was Jess, who was almost as infatuated with this archaic Gothic monstrosity as Bree was. Every time he mentioned selling the house, the pair of them looked at him as if he were a puppy kicker.

And then there was the crew. The local labor force was pretty much made up of cowboys. The boys were good—as Simon knew, anyone raised on a ranch was a jack-of-all-trades. He was paying them a premium wage, and the quality of work was the proof of their ability. The problem was sex. The crew were all men, which Bree seemed to like just fine, he thought darkly.

The boys had all taken to her. Simon couldn't turn a corner without catching some young pup trying to flirt with her, some old codger trying to make her laugh. Unless she was off someplace with Jess, she was in the thick of it, whipping those skinny legs around, bringing the men sandwiches or hauling tools, guessing where somebody needed a third hand.

Simon had realized from the start that she didn't realize what was going on. She figured they were all being "friendly." How a woman could travel across the country and remain so blasted naive was beyond him. Half those pups were drooling over her, and this was predator country. She seemed to have no comprehension what her southern drawl, slow eyes and little swish to her hips did to a man.

"It's not gonna come off, Daddy," Jessica said patiently.

He was on his fifth napkin, but all the dry paper seemed to accomplish was to move the sticky goo around. "What *is* this stuff?"

"Radishes."

"Radishes are not sticky."

"They must be. I didn't have any of those white cookies with the red jam inside," Jessica said virtuously.

He set the little one on the floor, knowing this was an ideal opportunity to give her a carefully worded talk about truth, trust and integrity, but for the moment he was just too distracted. "Honey, where's Bree?" he asked casually.

"With the guy."

"What guy?"

"The guy who cuts juice."

Jessica ran off. Simon spent another minute trying to wipe the confounded jam off his fingers and then abruptly trashed all the napkins. He had a thousand things to do. Upstairs, he'd sealed off a room of Fee's collections; he'd been nearly, but not completely, through the whole lot. He could check on the roofers, see how the painters were progressing downstairs, and the safety of the old electrical system was, of course, another problem. Simon sifted through his list of priorities and came up with the obvious conclusion.

Electricity was more important than anything else. The fuse box was in the furnace room. Before he even turned the corner, he heard the pair of voices.

"Aim it this way, will you, Bree?"

"Sure. This better?"

With the power off, the furnace room was gloomy-dark and shadowy. The battle-scarred washer and dryer were tucked in one corner. The workbench looked like a slab of prehistoric wood, a contrast to the spit-shiny pipes of the newly installed furnace. The decor didn't interest Simon. His complete attention riveted on the two bodies cuddled up close to the fuse box.

He'd come to know Tom. He was good. The boy not only had an electrician's license but had the practical experience of working at his father's side from the time he was knee-high. In looks he was tall and blondish, had a shy, slow grin and a cocky lope to his stride. Simon figured he was too young to shave. He couldn't be older than his mid-twenties. And the kid was never going to make thirty because he was going to be dead if he didn't quit following Bree around.

Bree was shoulders-brushing close, holding the flashlight so Tom could test the fuse in each circuit. She was on tiptoe, trying to carefully aim the light. Simon couldn't fault the boy for neglecting his job, but his eyes were a hell of a lot busier than his hands.

"You sure ain't from around here with that accent."

"I'm originally from Louisiana."

"No kidding? Bayous and magnolias and gumbo and all that?"

Bree chuckled. "All that."

"I guess there wouldn't be any chance you like to dance."

Again she laughed. "Is there sunshine in June?"

"I'm talking a barn dance now, nothing fancy. Community puts it on—a little country square dancing, a little rock and roll . . ."

Simon cleared a cough from his throat and jovially interrupted. "You should have said if you needed some help, Tom." Both sets of eyes swiveled toward him. He never once looked at Bree, just gently confiscated the flashlight from her hand and aimed it at the fuse box. "I imagine we can get this done fairly quickly. I'm no stranger to electricity. Like I said, you should have come to me if you needed any backup."

That's all he said. Nothing funny, nothing strange. Nothing at all to make Bree suddenly chuckle.

Simon had assumed they'd be eating cheese sandwiches for dinner. With no electricity or water for half the day, he couldn't see how she could cook.

Bree had blithely suggested that his life was far too dependent on electronic gadgets and breezily produced a dinner that could make a monk break a fast. The bread came out of the hearth oven, so did the mint-flavored potatoes. The pepper-blackened steak had been seared on a hibachi she'd set up outside.

The coals were still orange. Around seven, the temperature had just started to drop, and the big western sky was a deep, endless blue. Simon had no interest in poetic orange coals and blue skies, but the scenery was keeping his eyes off Bree.

His plate was on his lap, his back resting on one of the stone lions on the front porch. Bree was using the other stone lion as a backrest. Jessica had finished her dinner and was collecting fistfuls of wildflowers from the overgrown prairie his great-uncle had called a lawn. Simon still hadn't figured out why they were eating outside—the plumbing work was done, the kitchen reasonably back in shape—but Bree had apparently wanted to eat in the front field.

He'd catered to her whim.

He'd probably have catered to her if she'd set up the silverware and plates in the attic.

Methodically he buttered the last bite of roll. Her toes had strayed into his line of vision. Her feet were bare, and she'd painted her toenails Gypsy red. They matched her mouth, which wasn't painted at all. White jeans hugged her thighs, she was wearing a loose blue shirt that dipped in a V at her throat, and she'd tucked her hair behind her ears to get it out of her way, yet the wanton, silky strands caught every tuft of breeze.

She set down her empty plate with a lustily satisfied sigh, which Simon had regrettably discovered was how she did everything. Joyfully, lustfully and with a uniquely feminine joie de vivre that made him feel . . . nervous.

He stabbed the last piece of steak on his plate, thinking that he'd managed it—a quiet, peaceful meal. He'd sworn he wasn't going to say anything and he hadn't. When they talked about Jess, they did all right. When they got closer to any personal subject, he either ended up sounding like a pompous, judgmental jerk . . . or he shut down fast.

Bree didn't know how he felt about her. She never would. She was sunshine and sass. He rooted his life in responsibilities. She was winsome, open, a fresh spark of life—a spark he'd long lost. Simon could write a book on inhibitions. There was no excuse—none—for the embarrassing attraction he felt for her. When they were together, the tension accelerated, picking up momentum like a tumbleweed in a high wind. He had, thank heavens, complete control over it.

"Well..." Bree stood up and stretched. "I guess I'd better go in and change clothes."

And out it came, the one subject he'd sworn to avoid. "You're not really going out with that boy. You don't know him from Adam."

Soft blue eyes browsed his expression. He had the nasty feeling she was amused. "Tom is hardly a boy, Simon. He's a very nice man."

"You don't know that."

"He's been around the house for a week. I know him well enough. It's just a dance. What'd you think of the steak—too much pepper?"

"The steak was wonderful," he said flatly. "What time is he picking you up?"

"He isn't. I'm driving myself and meeting him there."

"See?" he snapped.

"See what?"

"If you set it up so that you have independent transportation, you weren't sure what you were getting into."

"True," she murmured.

"What do you mean, true?"

"I mean that you're right. I didn't want to be picked up. I wanted my own wheels. Maybe he drinks. Maybe he has more than a dance in mind. I don't think so or I wouldn't be going, but occasionally I'm capable of being cautious."

She patted his shoulder affectionately, as if she were a hundred years old and he were a schoolboy. He was thirty-five years old. *She* was the relative baby, and as long as he thought of himself as her Dutch uncle, he could ultimately master this tension business.

"You don't seriously have any objection to my being gone for a few hours, do you?" she asked him mildly.

"Of course not."

"If you needed me to do something—"

"I don't *need* you to do a damn thing. You've been doing slave labor, which I have repeatedly told you is unnecessary."

"I thought," she said gently, "that you'd honestly like me out of your hair for a while. You can't want to spend another evening with my beating you at another game of chess."

Simon was too much a gentleman to tell her that the only reason she beat him at chess was because she made completely wild, unpredictable moves.

"Think of it, *cher.* A whole evening of peace and quiet. You have no idea how much you're going to enjoy it," she told him cheerfully, and abruptly swiveled her head around toward Jessica. "I need to talk to your daughter."

Momentarily he was equally distracted by the flamboyant streak of color cartwheeling in the yard. "I wish you would. I've tried, but it doesn't do any good. I can't believe what clothes she picks out to put on her body—"

Bree chuckled. "She picks out what she likes. What's the harm?"

"She's four years old and wearing earrings."

"This is a major problem? She's into glamour this month. She'll undoubtedly be into frogs next month."

It was beyond Simon why he found her advice so reassuring when the woman didn't even have the sense to wear shoes. "You don't think it's a little... abnormal... that she goes around with more makeup than a circus clown?"

"*Normal* is such a silly word. She's healthy and happy and wonderfully independent. Unless you absolutely have to, I'd just let her be...although, on the subject of makeup, I have to admit that your daughter and I are about to come to blows." Bree dusted off the back of her jeans and took the steps down to the yard. "That little turkey filched my blue eye shadow, and I need it tonight."

Simon watched her hips sashay toward Jessica, saw the breeze spill through her cloud of dark hair and thought she was right. He needed an evening without her around.

Time after dinner was reserved for Jess, but once his urchin was asleep, Bree generally coaxed him into the kitchen and set up the chessboard. Chess between consenting adults was an innocuous way to spend an evening. Or it should be, if he could keep his mind on the game and off that soft red mouth, those long, long legs and lambent blue eyes. Everything about her was sexy. She probably brushed her teeth passionately, he thought dryly.

Simon reached for his iced tea. When he pigeonholed his feelings as plain old lust, he didn't feel half as nervous. He was too humiliatingly aware that he probably couldn't please her in bed. A woman with all that passion and energy and sensuality?

At the moment, though, she'd caught Jessica's hands and was swinging his daughter around. Both were laughing. Bree had brought the incredible gift of laughter into their lives, but in a rare instant the light would catch her eyes a certain way and he'd see something. A lonesomeness, a longing, a yearning... and hurt. A woman's wounding scars, not a girl's. And he'd stupidly think that she, too, needed someone.

Maybe she does need someone, Courtland, he told himself. But it isn't you. While Bree was here, she was under his care. Simon was determined to think of himself as her Dutch uncle if it killed him. Yet the idle, stray thought dawdled through his mind that if she came home with her lipstick smudged, a fingernail broken, the least sign that that boy had laid an unwanted hand on her—he'd be sorry he was ever born.

Bree closed the VW's door so quietly that a mouse couldn't have heard it. Her watch claimed it was almost two. No clouds marred the spectacularly star-speckled sky, but the night temperature was cold enough to freeze her tush.

Still, she took a moment to balance against the VW's hood and slip off her high heels. Her bare feet promptly froze on the gritty, cold ground, but she didn't care. She'd danced her feet off. Her toes needed wriggling room, and heaven knew, her head needed clearing. Two beers. A record for her. The barn had been packed, hot and smoky, and the music wild. Tom was a fantastic dancer, and she'd had pent-up energy to burn. She'd let it all go.

It hadn't helped.

Hooking one finger around the straps of her shoes, she tiptoed up the porch steps to the stone lions. Tom was...adorable. A little cocky, but that was mostly show. He was soft-spoken and sweet, and she'd known two hours ahead that he was working up his courage for the end of the evening. She hadn't sent him any mixed signals, but he was a man, and a man was always going to find out if there was a chance he could get lucky. She drew the line at a kiss, but yes, she'd kissed him. It wasn't terrible, it wasn't awful, but she could have gotten the same emotional effect from kissing a floppy-pawed puppy.

So that hadn't worked, either.

She'd counted on the evening to force some perspective on her feelings for Simon. It should have helped to get out, to kick up her heels with an unquestionably nice guy and dance until she dropped. She'd never traveled anyplace where she hadn't involved herself in the local people, the local color. She should have had a wonderful time.

She'd been miserable. Nothing was the same without that horrible man. Six hours with no one to argue with, no one to sneak up on her with his too-clear perceptions and value judgments—she should have been thrilled. Did Courtland even want her? No. Did she want her heart more involved with Courtland? No. Had he once laid a finger on her, indicating desire or caring or any real feeling? No. At least not when he was awake. So why was a quiet walk in the dark or a chess game or a bickering match at breakfast more exciting with that damned man than anything she did without him?

That isn't a tough question, Reynaud. You need a straitjacket. A little time in one of those places that has lots of trees and fenced grounds and itsy-bitsy bars on the windows.

Wincingly quiet, wary of waking anyone, she turned the key in the lock. It creaked a bit, but not much. Painstakingly slowly, she turned the doorknob. Simon must have left a light on in the parlor, because the hall was dark but not blue-black. She tiptoed in, carefully closed the door. Yawned. Turned. And screamed.

"It's just me. Not a ghost."

Her hand still on her heart, she hissed, "You scared the life out of me. What are you still doing up?"

"You could have had a flat tire."

"Simon, I've changed five million flat tires in my time." He was sitting halfway up the stairs, hunched forward with his arms hooked over his bent knees. His shirtsleeves were cuffed up and his hair looked disheveled, and right off Bree guessed he was wired. The signs were unmistakable. When Simon was overtired, he'd challenge a grizzly bear, then turn around and snap at a lion. "You worked tonight," she accused him.

"The electricity was off half the day. Of course I worked."

"And you didn't have your cognac."

His eyes zeroed in on hers, as bright and dark as razor-sharp beads. "Reynaud, could you try and get it through your head that I can survive without a nightly cognac? Where did you even get the idea that I was a drinker? I've gone whole months without—''

''I'll get just a little one. For both of us,'' she said swiftly. The kitchen was pitch-dark and the sudden overhead light harsh enough to make her eyes dilate. She spilled a few sips of the French brandy into a snifter for herself and poured a full water glass to the brim for him.

He was still there. On the seventh step. She gathered the loose folds of her calico skirt and perched on the fourth. he gave her a spit-polish black look when she handed him the glass, but he took a gulp. It wasn't wise to stay—the lonely hall and dim light made an oddly intimate oasis of the stairs—but it wouldn't take him long to finish the cognac. It never did.

''Did you have a good time?''

''Wonderful,'' she raved.

''So you're glad you went.''

''Tremendously glad.'' She whisked him a determined smile, then wished she hadn't. A woman could hardly stay put together after six hours of dancing, yet Bree made her aware that her nose was shiny, her cheeks wind flushed and her hair had long escaped its token pins. He studied her so intently that her pulse started to ricochet, and it worsened when he concentrated on her mouth.

''Did he give you any trouble?''

The devil made her say it. ''Nothing that wasn't enormous fun to handle.''

Simon sighed. Loudly. ''The only reason I asked is that he's working here. And if he gave you a hard time, he'll be off the property tomorrow.''

''Simon?''

"I'm listening."

"Try and remember that I'm twenty-seven, would you? If Tom gave me a hard time, he wouldn't be on the property tomorrow because he'd be black-and-blue and probably suffering smashed ribs." She saw his lips twitch and felt piqued. Simon was hopelessly protective of anyone and anything in his wake. She leaned back to scratch a sudden itch against the spokes of the banister. She was awfully tired of being put in that lump with the rest of the million people he took care of. "Do you like to dance?"

He swirled the liquid in his glass, but she never saw him take a second sip. "'Like to,'" he said dryly, "is fairly irrelevant. I don't dance. Because I was never any good at it."

"I'll bet you'd be good at dirty dancing."

"I beg your pardon?"

"I guess the style started with the movie, but frankly I think it's the men who made sure it stuck around. You don't have to know a bunch of intricate dance steps to pull it off—you just have to know how to make love. It's all in the rhythm, the emotion of the music—"

"Reynaud, how the hell much have you had to drink?"

She tipped the cognac glass to her lips and sipped. "Plenty," she assured him, but she knew better. Two beers over six thirsty hours of physical exercise was hardly enough to affect her. It wasn't liquor making her feel reckless. It was Simon. "We have a saying in my part of the country," she said blithely. "*Laissez le bon temps rouler.* Let the good times roll. If the world's going to end, there's nothing you can do about it, so you might as well live it up, soak up the sunshine and laugh while you can. Would you like me to show you how to dirty dance?''

''No.'' He stole the brandy snifter from her hand and set it behind him. ''You're going to bed, Bree. Now.''

She needed to disappear, all right, but not for the reason Simon thought. She wasn't tipsy; she'd been teasing him. But at an embarrassingly private level, she'd meant the invitation.

All evening, every time the band played rhythm and blues, she had imagined dancing with Simon. Not in a crowd. He'd never like a crowd. But the hall was dark and the hour was late, and maybe he'd be stiff at first, but not if the music was right, not if the woman was right. The dancing partner she'd imagined hadn't been the tie-wearing Courtland or her sleepwalking phantom lover...but a blend of both. A man who could be.

At least with the right woman. Someone needed to pull down Simon's emotional house of cards, but in a hundred ways Bree knew—in a thousand ways he'd told her—that it wasn't her. Abruptly she stood up and backed down the steps to fetch her shoes. ''Did Jessica go to sleep all right?''

He responded to the prosaic question with a ''Fine'' and said nothing else until she'd climbed back up the stairs to a level with him. His hand suddenly curled around her wrist. Unwanted nerves shivered through her as bright and hot as sparklers. ''Bree?''

He released her wrist.

''You didn't have a good time. You're as touchy as a hot fuse,'' he said quietly. ''I don't know why you went out with that boy, but it had nothing to do with 'letting the good times roll.' Something's eating at you, and if you need help, I'm here. I don't give a damn if we don't get along. I'd be there. You understand?''

"No," she whispered, but she suddenly felt as raw as if a sensitive nerve were exposed to air. If his perception was unsettling, the stroke of compassion in his voice was even more so.

"Maybe you've been on the road all these months because you have a wild, woolly urge for adventure. And maybe... someone hurt you. Badly. Like in the back seat of that Buick?''

"Buick?" she asked blankly, but the vague reference came back to her with cringing clarity. About a dozen nights ago, her impulsive streak had gotten the better of her and she'd spit out something about the incident when she was sixteen. At the time, she'd only meant to imply that she had about a million years of experience taking care of herself, but it had never occurred to her that Simon would remember it... or that he'd leap to the wrong kind of conclusion.

For a sharp, dark moment, he almost scared her. All he was doing was sitting midway on the staircase in your basic two-in-the-morning dark hall. But his eyes were fierce and intent, his mouth a flat line. And her mind formed the crazy image of his going back through the chapters of her life and finding a tall, red-haired boy to tear limb from limb.

"I was never hurt, *cher,* not like you mean," she said softly. "There was no abuse, no threat, no rape. Nothing like that, ever, in my life. Any trouble I ever had—of any kind—I asked for.''

When he didn't respond, she zipped up a few more steps to the turn on the landing, hesitated, and then briefly hung over the railing. "Don't forget your cognac before you go to sleep, Courtland," she called down to him.

It took very few minutes for Bree to strip off her clothes, tug on a nightshirt and pull out the dormer bed in the third-story tower room.

A week before at breakfast, in a moment of stubbornness, she'd announced that she was claiming the room as hers. Simon had expressed no interest in where she slept—the house had a million rooms—but it had mattered to Bree. For one thing, she couldn't spend every night hiding out in different bedrooms trying to outwit a sleepwalker who had every room key anyway, and for another, she was tired of strange beds.

She wanted—needed—a place to call her own. From downstairs, she'd filched a Chinese lacquered screen and a fringed rug. The belongings were only temporarily hers, but when Bree was here she felt as if she were in a castle's sanctuary, high up with a marvelous window view of a landscape Rapunzel would have loved.

Unlike Rapunzel, however, Bree wasn't inclined to let down her long hair for any gentlemen callers.

She booby-trapped the room every night. Going to the trouble tonight seemed silly—Simon hadn't strayed near her room in a week; the hour was incredibly late, and he'd surely sleep soundly after that cognac. Still, it wasn't as though setting up her booby trap were complicated. First, she tacked a strong nylon string waist-high, then piled up a barricade of pil-

lows—that way if he fell, he wouldn't hurt himself—
and last, she hooked an antique cowbell to the string.
Not much in this life was louder than a cowbell.

No one, no way, no how was getting near her bed in
the middle of the night without her hearing him
first . . . and there was a level where Bree didn't care if
her booby trap was silly. Day by day, Simon was less
stiff, more open. Feelings sneaked through when he
forgot to guard them. Tonight, for that brief moment
on the stairs, she had a glimpse of how he might be
with a woman he cared about: perceptive, protective,
there for her in any time of trouble.

He'd moved Bree. She didn't want to be moved. Her
feelings for Simon were already as unsettled as a keg
of dynamite, and she refused to fall in love with another man who only temporarily needed her around.
In a little less than two weeks, his ex-wife would show
up for Jess. If it took cowbells for her to sleep rest-
fully until then, she'd use cowbells.

She fell into bed and blindly grabbed for the sheets
and comforter. Faster than the switch of a light, she
was asleep.

Seven

———

The cowbells failed.

Of course it was possible that Bree hadn't heard them. She'd fallen so fast, so hard and into such a deep sleep that she probably wouldn't have heard a brass band.

Maybe no sound could have wakened her . . . but Simon's touch did. Like the other times, he did nothing to frighten her. A burglar's movements were stealthy, furtive. Simon slid into bed as naturally as he'd seek a familiar lover. His hand tucked around her ribs and rested just under her breasts. The supple wall of his chest nuzzled against her back until they fit like two puzzle pieces. He shifted her hair away from her nape as if he were awake, as if he'd done it a thousand times, and then his head dropped onto the pillow. This close, they didn't need two pillows. She could smell his clean, warm skin. She could feel the even sough of his breath on the back of her neck.

She could feel her whole female body coming to zinging, stinging sensual life, and she turned in his arms with a building feeling of despair.

Simon had tucked the comforter around her yet failed to cover himself. Moonlight caught the sweep of short, stubby lashes on his cheek and a boyish yank of hair on his brow. His eyes were closed, his breathing deep and even, and the emotion hit her low and sharp and irrevocably.

Neither the booby traps nor the tough lectures had saved her. It was too late; she was already in love with him. Not just Simon, but Courtland. Not just her ardent sleepwalker, but the man who'd waited for her on the stairs tonight, the same man who assumed he was hardened against all emotion.

Simon felt too much, not too little. Instinctively she pulled the cover over his bare shoulder. Her fingertips stroked his cheek and pushed back, so gently, that yank of hair. Her grandmother used to tell her stories about the *feu follet*—the evil spirit that pursued its victims and caused them to lose their way in the swamps. Bree didn't know the nature of Simon's *feu follet,* but her heart recognized a man who'd lost his way.

She sank back against the pillow and just looked at him. Nothing could soften his strong features, but the harsh lines of control disappeared in sleep. He valued that control; she'd never seen it shaken. Only at night did his defenses come tumbling down, and only then, because even Simon was vulnerable in his sleep.

She refused to wake him. Jessica mustn't find him here in the morning, but Bree could force herself to stay awake for hours. Someone had to guard his sleep, watch over and protect him. How many of the last nights had he wandered the dark rooms alone?

Not tonight. If she had to pinch herself every ten minutes, she was going to keep Simon safe and warm tonight. He was so desperate for rest. She'd never seen him look so young, so at peace, so completely unguarded and innocent....

"Damn."

Bree's eyes popped open faster than sprung wires. A groggy voice seemed to be coming from a spot just above her head. It wasn't a happy voice. In fact it reeked, just a tad, with horror.

For about two seconds, they both lay frozen. Her gaze locked on his Adam's apple, which seemed to be located about three inches from her nose. One of his arms was crushed under her. His other hand rather loosely cradled her fanny. Her bare fanny. Her nightshirt had ridden up to her waist, and her right leg was trapped between his. He was wearing underpants. She wasn't. Something warm and hard was throbbing against her upper thigh, which they both seemed to realize simultaneously.

She started scuffling at the same instant he did. She didn't mean to kick him; she was just trying to pull her nightshirt down. And Simon couldn't have meant to drag a hand over her breasts; it was just that arms and legs and covers were so tangled.

"If you'd just calm down and let me—"

"I was calm until you jabbed me in the ribs—"

"I didn't mean to jab you in the ribs. I was trying to protect my—"

"I know what you were trying to protect, *cher*. I didn't mean to kick you. I was trying to help—"

"Don't help anymore, all right? Or at least not with your knees. Look, if you'd just stay still—"

"I can hardly just lie here when your hand is on my—"

"Bree. Has this happened before?"

At the precise instant he asked the question, she happened to have a sheet draped over her head. She didn't do anything to remove it. Through the north window, the sky was beginning to lighten, and darkness was much easier to handle.

There were ample electrical sparks in the room to cause a brush fire. Spontaneous combustion. Nobody would need a match. Bree wasn't sure which was worse. The nasty, delicious, forbidden tingles shooting through her because of their intimate tussle. Or the guilty knowledge that her responsiveness to Simon was shamefully familiar. To her. Not him.

In Louisiana, unlike South Dakota, there were wonderful big swamps of quicksand a woman could sink into on occasions like this.

There was nothing so handily concealing here. Simon peeled down the sheet, determined to get a look at her face. His skin was as flushed as hers, his hair just as disheveled, and unless she was mistaken, he was having his own problems with a guilt attack, although not for the same reason.

"How many times have I bothered you in the night?"

"You didn't bother me. It wasn't like that." He'd obviously been praying for a completely different answer. She saw his eyes squeeze closed, the muscles ripple in his jaw. Immediately he started to lurch out of bed, only to change his mind and grab the sheet. Simon could be pretty Victorian, but she doubted that his near nudity bothered him. He'd snatched the sheet to conceal his arousal. "Simon, it's okay—"

"*Nothing* is okay. I don't believe I did this to you." He dragged a hand through his hair, avoiding her eyes. "Something happened when I was fourteen. That's when it started. The idiotic sleepwalking. Only I thought it was completely over. I haven't had the problem in at least ten years. What on earth is *that*..."

Bree lifted her head to see the pile of debris by the door. The pillows were neatly piled, her string nicely coiled, the cowbell stacked on top of the heap. It gave her an excuse to smile. Maybe humor would chase away the raw, dark, mortified look in his eyes. Wouldn't it ease his mind to think she'd never been shaken up by his sleepwalking? "You're even tidy in your sleep, *cher,* and I really think you should consider a second career as a thief. You can get through locked doors, not only anticipate but apparently disarm booby traps, and you have the tracking nose of a hound because I tried changing rooms a while ago—"

"I must have scared you."

"Maybe a little."

"Well, at least I never climbed into bed with you before—"

"Heavens, no," she lied swiftly.

Too swiftly. He leaned over, balancing on an elbow, and turned her chin in his direction. Nerves collected in the pit of her stomach. This wasn't at all like being in bed with his sleepwalking alter ego. Asleep, Simon was always nice. Gentle. Relatively obedient and wonderfully handleable.

This was more like finding herself with a tawny-headed lion. He was far too naked and she felt far too exposed, and there was a natural hunter's intensity in his eyes. His prey was the truth. He was going to have it. "Did I do more than climb into bed with you?"

"Heavens, n—"

"Reynaud." She understood that he was demanding a straight answer, but for a moment she couldn't think. His thumb gently stroked her jawbone—he probably didn't realize what he was doing—and until that moment she certainly hadn't realized that he wanted her. The real Simon, not her midnight caller. The tough, cold Courtland who wasted no time on emotion at the moment had a badly trembling hand and eyes so dark they made her shiver.

"Nothing happened," she assured him.

His voice was rough and low. "There's a level where I know that. We couldn't have made love. Believe me, Bree, I'd know if I made love with you." Again, he stroked the fragile bone of her jaw. "What I want to know is if I did anything to embarrass or offend you."

"No."

"Don't look someone in the eyes when you lie, honey. You can't fib worth a damn and it only makes it worse. And the way you're looking at me..." He took a long breath and hissed a swearword. A range of expressions crossed his face. One of them even included humor. "I feel like someone threw me a birthday party and I missed the present. I was a kid when I used to sleepwalk, but believe me, the nature of this particular problem never came up before. Bree, I don't understand why you didn't do the obvious. Shake me, slap me, do whatever you had to do to wake me up—''

"I was...afraid to," she admitted.

Perception harshened his features, and his scowl was fierce. "You thought I'd hurt you? Take advantage?"

"No," she promised him, and closed her eyes. The total truth burned deeper than she wanted him to see. She knew Simon now. He'd never hurt her. The real fears her phantom lover aroused came from inside Bree. Her whole nature was to offer the shirt off her back, but somewhere she'd hoped to find the one man who wouldn't take it. The man who came to her in the night had never taken advantage of her vulnerability. He could have. She'd have made love with him. There was a terrible chance she'd have done anything, anyway, anyhow for the Simon of the haunted, dark eyes.

But the situation was more complicated now. She hadn't known that Courtland, too, was fighting chemistry, or that being this physically close would feel like gasoline thrown on an already searing fire. She had to remember that desire wasn't love. She had to remember that Simon didn't even believe in love.

"Bree—"

"You mentioned that something happened when you were fourteen. What was it?" she asked swiftly.

Apparently she couldn't have chosen a more instant mood changer. His eyes blanked of emotion, and he leaned back. "My father died."

"Lord, I'm sorry."

He seemed to go to another place. "He was a good man. A far better man than I'll ever be." Dawn light had slowly seeped into the room until rays of gold caught in his hair. The radiator clanked when the furnace suddenly turned on. It was the only sound in the room. "I was the oldest. Four younger kids and my mother. I can still remember it. The funeral. Everyone crying their eyes out—except for me. I wasn't crying. I was sweating blood wondering how the hell I was going to get them all fed." His gaze suddenly met hers, challenging, hard. "Does that tell you anything about my character?"

"Yes," she whispered.

"I was a cold son of a bitch even when I was fourteen."

It was as if he wanted to be sure she knew, but that wasn't the message she heard. Inside, she ached for him.

"I loved my father, Reynaud, but he left six people without a buck to buy a quart of milk. You think I mourned him?"

"I think," she said softly, "that you never gave yourself the chance to mourn him." But she could see he wasn't listening. Simon seemed determined to classify his character for her. Later, it would occur to her that he was trying to ensure she knew she was safe with him.

"They all think I'm a bastard. They're all right. Liz said I was too hard to have any feelings. She was right, too. I'm not a *nice* man, Bree, and whatever happened when I was sleepwalking in the middle of the night—forget it."

She got the message. If by some disgusting twist of fate he'd been gentle or kind or, God forbid, passionate, she wasn't to worry that he was prey to such reprehensible character traits during the day.

The dawdling thought crossed her mind that she'd like to throw herself on top of him and kiss him silly.

Perhaps luckily, she had no chance to give in to the dangerous impulse. Simon glanced at the clock and immediately swung his legs over the side of the bed. The hour was only six, but both of them realized Jessica could waken at any time. Bree knew he had to leave, yet she couldn't resist a few more questions.

"You said you started sleepwalking when you were fourteen. Surely your family realized—"

"Oh, they realized. One time they found me walking down the road at three in the morning. My sleepwalking drove the whole clan nuts. Eventually they packed me off to a doctor."

"And?"

He looked around the room as if to find something to cover himself. There wasn't anything. He stood up, anyway. "And I had a complete physical. Passed it like a marine, so that was a zero. Then they tried sending me off to a shrink who wanted to talk to me about 'unresolved dreams.' Another zero. I didn't have any half-baked 'unresolved dreams.' As a last shot, I tried a so-called sleep clinic."

"They found nothing, either?" Bree trailed the so straight line of his spine, not with her finger, just with her eyes, thinking that she'd never met a man with more unresolved dreams. Dreams he'd never given a chance. Or couldn't.

"Yeah, they did." Simon's tone was dry. "Apparently a lot of sleepwalkers have this little electrical thing happen in their brain. It's not something 'wrong.' It's not something they fix like an illness. It's just something different in one person from another, like some people have blue eyes and some have brown. Sleepwalking isn't even unusual, and for most people it's no big deal."

"So they didn't help you?" He wasn't wasting any time moving toward the door.

"Sure, they helped. They told me to tie myself to a bed. It worked then and it'll work again." He opened the door and turned to look at her one last time. The only time she'd seen his eyes look that haunted before had been in the dark of the night. His gaze fixed on her against the pillows, her sleep-tumbled hair, her bare throat, her mouth. Whatever emotion was in his expression—longing? desire?—she was quite positive he'd deny it to the death.

"And if that rope doesn't work, I'll try something else. The point, Bree, is that you won't have to worry about it again. I'll give you all the house keys. Not that my Uncle Fee was eccentric, but for some insane reason there are dozens of them and all of them function as skeleton keys. What's the point of locking doors if any key'll get you in? Anyway, if you have all the keys, you won't have to worry about my ever bothering you again."

When he was gone, Bree propped her elbow on her knee and cupped her chin in her palm. *Thank you so much for relieving my mind, Courtland. I have a much better picture of the situation now, and everything's hunky-dory.*

What a crock. Her thumbnail was just long enough to chew. She thought about Simon having to tie himself into a bed and felt sick. She thought about a young boy who'd had to grow up too fast, who had never once had a break from people depending on him, even when he got married. She thought about unresolved dreams. She thought about how carefully Simon had protected her from believing he might care. She thought about the way he'd looked at her.

And she thought about his adorable tush.

And then she quit chewing on her thumbnail and climbed out of bed.

"What's this, Bree?"

"*Couche couche.*" Bree poured the little one a glass of milk but kept one eye on Simon. Freshly showered, freshly shaved, freshly brushed, Simon had retreated behind a *Wall Street Journal* with a mug of coffee the moment he walked into the kitchen. Not that the idea of any further conversation embarrassed him, but when she'd turned around from the stove, a genie had silently left an enormous ring of house keys by her coffee. She was welcome to be chatelaine of the castle. As long as he didn't ever have to talk about what had happened last night again as long as he lived.

"I thought we had that two days ago. This isn't the same thing."

"That was cush-cush, *chère.* This is *couche couche.* It's like a cereal. Trust me, it's terrible for you—almost as bad as Captain Cracko."

Jessica took a nibble off the spoon as if she were testing for poison. Reassured then, she dove in. "What are we going to do today?"

"A little later in the morning, we're going to take your daddy on an adventure in the Badlands." Bree heard the newspaper crackle restlessly. She was busy swiping the counter at the sink. "I thought we'd climb some upside-down mountains, maybe go calling on some prairie dogs and have a picnic by your secret hideout."

"Sounds great!"

"It sounds—" the monk irritably peered over the rim of his monastery "—like a typically imaginative Reynaud-type outing. Affecting two. Not three."

"Chaque chien a son jour," she murmured, and then most apologetically, "You're going, Simon."

"As you're well aware..." The newspaper had to go down when his daughter sneaked under it to climb onto his lap. Jess was carrying the bowl of couche couche and a spoon and a dangerously splashing glass of orange juice. Simon juggled fast. "I don't have any free time. I have several calls coming in from Boston that I can't afford to miss. I'm not finished with Fee's collections. The painting crew is scheduled to move upstairs today—"

"It's a shame, I know," Bree said sympathetically, "but they'll all have to function without you. You're going."

"It's not possible." Simon said the words slowly, as if hoping that clear enunciation would get through someone's sluggish brain cells. "You've been around here long enough to realize that I have too many responsibilities to—"

"Yes. I realize. Which is exactly the point. You're going, Simon."

* * *

He couldn't be here, Simon told himself. He just couldn't be.

He'd been a good father. He'd driven the two of them to the Sage Creek Basin; he'd hiked five million miles off the road carrying three pairs of binoculars and a doll; he'd sat patiently until the two had had their fill of watching prairie dogs. Truthfully, the little critters were kind of cute—less than a foot tall, blondish brown and busier than gossips. Some nibbled grass, some nuzzled and chased each other, and a few apparently had the job of lookouts. At the first sign of a red-tailed hawk, the lookouts barked like little dogs, warning the whole town to dive underground.

Bree had loved it, Jess had been enchanted and even Simon was willing to admit that the outing had been fun. But enough was enough.

He had a million things to do. The Boston contract was coming to a head. Someone in the family would call with an emergency—they always did—and he wouldn't be there. The master bedroom could easily end up little-girl pink unless he was around to supervise the painting crew. And unless he finished cataloging the last of Fee's collections, he was going to be stuck forever with that radiator-clanking, archaic, unsalable albatross of a house in the middle of nowhere.

Instead of being where he needed to be—where he *had* to be—he was lying belly-down on some crumbly dirt, the sun soporifically beaming down on his head, with forty pounds of excited four-year-old bouncing on his back.

Bree had the binoculars. His daughter took a look through her own pair and exchanged a knowing glance with Bree.

"They're coming," Jess said grimly.

"Don't worry about a thing. I'm ready for them."

"You sure you got enough ammo?"

"Plenty. You just protect your dad."

"Get your head *down,* Daddy."

There was nothing in sight. When he'd driven back from Sage Creek, Simon had mistakenly assumed he was free to return to work, but no. The girls insisted that he "had to see" Jessica's hideout. Said famed hideout was a *long* half-mile hike from the house and was nothing more than a plain old butte sticking up in the middle of nowhere. They'd climbed the steep side of the knoll by catching handfuls of scrub grass for purchase. The top was as flat as a board, and Simon had expected a view. The only thing on the other side was a gully wash—an eroded clay stream bed, baked to cracking.

Bree, being Bree, had told Jessica it was filled with gold.

And Bree, being Bree, now stood up, pretended to spit in both palms and raised an imaginary rifle to her shoulder. Her thumb flicked off the safety, and she squinted into the sight. "Good grief. There's a dozen of them. Look at that cloud of dust behind their horses. For heaven's sake, keep your daddy safe, Jess."

"I got him covered."

"They're coming in range. All of them. Jesse James. Billy the Kid. Old man Clanton. Doc Holiday...." Bree's finger pulled the rifle trigger in rapid succession. Jess made the "bangs."

Simon buried his face in his hands, trying the best he could to muffle his laughter.

Eventually Jessica pried open his fingers, one at a time. "It's all right, Daddy. Don't be scared. We're safe. They're all gone."

"I see. They're all...dead?"

"Nobody's dead, Daddy. Bree and me would die before killing anything. We just want to scare them off. They want the gold in our creek," Jessica explained. "I'll get you some. Then you'll understand."

His daughter tumbled down the slick slope on her gold hunt. Faster than her imaginary trigger finger, Bree changed back to an adult again—a transition that always disarmed him. Efficiently she collected the last of the lunch debris in a basket and flopped down near his side.

"How do you do it?" he murmured. "Think up all that stuff with her?"

"A sick imagination?"

"I think I'd call it a special gift for children."

She wouldn't take the compliment. "I'm afraid it's going to take her a while to find gold," she admitted dryly.

"A while? From the look of that creek bed, we're going to be here until the next dinosaur age."

She chuckled. "Jess discovered this place on one of our long walks. She fell in love on sight—heaven knows why. I have her most ardent promise that she'll never try to walk here alone, but it has me a little worried. Your daughter's promises are worth as much as—''

''Three-dollar bills?''

They kept talking for a while, but it was desultory conversation and Simon lost track of the context. She'd rolled onto her back with her arms behind her head, soaking up the sun with her eyes closed. Eyelashes as dark as smoke shaded her cheeks. Her breasts disappeared when she was lying flat, and the maron necklace she wore caught the glint of the sun on her bare throat.

He searched his mind but could find no specific reason why she stirred him up like no other woman ever had.

''Can you smell it?'' she murmured.

''Smell what?''

''The sunlight.''

He found a blade of grass to poke between his teeth, not bothering to answer. There was, of course, no answer. You couldn't smell sunlight, just as there was no Jesse James gunfight nor a duchess serving high tea.

It was just Bree. The way she thought. The way she was.

Certain aspects of her character never failed to aggravate him. Her attitude about money, for one. Because she refused to take payment for staying, he'd had new tires put on her car. She'd thrown a fit. He'd taped a significant amount of cash under her dash, not expecting her to find it until she was gone. She'd found it and thrown another fit.

Simon tried to think of another human being in his life who didn't want something from him, didn't need something from him, didn't demand something from him. And couldn't.

"If Jess doesn't bring the gold soon," Bree murmured, "I'm afraid the sun is going to put me to sleep."

"Probably all that gunplay wore you out." She chuckled, a throaty, sleepy, sexy sound that played on his nerves like a fine sonata. "Go on and nap. I have my eye on Jess."

It wasn't quite true. Jessica could wander for a quarter mile and still be in his peripheral vision, and there was no trouble she could get into. He had nothing more critical to do than concentrate his complete attention on Bree.

He was going nuts not knowing what had happened when he'd been sleepwalking. He wanted to know in exact detail. He wanted to know if he'd kissed her . . . what she tasted like, how she'd responded. He wanted to know if he'd caressed the small, white swell of her breasts. He wanted to know if she'd liked it. He wanted to know if she'd been naked.

On second thought, he didn't want to know if she'd been naked. If he'd missed being in bed with Bree naked, he'd take poison.

He bit the stalk of grass clean in two and closed his eyes. Come on, Courtland. How many times are you going to put yourself through this? he asked himself.

A relationship with Bree wasn't possible. He knew that.

The only person he'd ever been close to was his father. He'd loved his dad, irrevocably, unconditionally. Sam Courtland had been a warm, generous, effusively affectionate man—everything Simon admired and wanted to be. But Sam's unexpected death had left his family destitute, and disillusionment had hit Simon hard at fourteen. An unbearable grief had turned to anger. Talk was cheap. So was love. Neither fed a family of five.

Simon had dug in his heels, refused to let anyone close, and worked. Poverty had snapped at their heels for years. If he'd been less hard, less driving, less determined, those teeth would have snapped him up. He'd always had too many people to care for to let that happen.

He had money now. Maybe . . . too much. Long before he met Bree, the rat-race pace of his life had started to gnaw and chafe, but the nature of man he'd become was carved in relative stone. He knew how to work, to protect, to secure. But he didn't know how to reach out. Not anymore. He had no idea how to woo a woman and had nothing to offer one—unless she was interested in money.

Bree didn't give sweet patooties for his money. She wanted him. Sexually. Simon would have to be deaf or blind not to pick up those so subtle, so unconscious female vibrations she sent out. But long-term, she wasn't likely to want a confirmed, staid workaholic. And short-term . . . he knew how he was in bed. Careful, considerate, controlled. Some women appreciated those qualities, but Simon had a pretty good idea that the Gypsy needed a wilder lover. It would take a man of passion and spirit to keep her.

That wasn't him.

Next to him, she stirred. A whisper of wind sent a stray curl of hair across her cheek. Without thinking, he leaned closer to push it away. His fingertips brushed the soft skin of her cheek, and he could feel every muscle in his body tighten and ache.

She was so beautiful, so full of laughter and life. Like a hunger gnawing inside him, he wished he had a way to tell her what she'd come to mean to him. It wasn't that he wanted anything from Bree or had any unrealistic expectations about the future. But when he was with her, he felt more open, more alive. When he was with her, he found himself remembering the dreams that had once really mattered to him. When he was with her, he even had the cockamamy notion that he could smell the sunlight.

Her eyelashes drifted open while his palm was still on her cheek. Blue eyes, as dangerous and alluring as love, focused on his face.

He jerked back quickly. "There was a bee," he said flatly. "I thought it was going to sting you."

She looked around. There were miles of ranch grasses in every direction, but no flowers in sight. "Imagine," she murmured. "A bee in this part of the country."

He came that close to kissing the sassy grin off her face. But he wasn't quite that brave—not then—not with his daughter scrambling over the top of the knoll with her fists full of gold.

Eight

————

"I have to warn you, Reynaud, that's a dangerous opening."

"Yes, Simon."

"You have a wonderful instinct for the game, but you don't *plan*. If you would just organize ahead, consider several moves in advance—"

"Yes, Simon." Bree brushed her last nail with Flaming Scarlet and redeposited the brush in the nail polish bottle. The polish would easily dry before Simon made his next move.

The hour was ten, and the whole house dark except for their private corner of the parlor. She'd set up the antique marble chessboard on the Bombay chest by the hearth. Yellow flames sizzled and spat in the fireplace, and the only other light was the ruby-globed lamp next to Simon's wing chair.

The walls were a fresh ivory now, the debris and clutter gone. The floor-to-ceiling velvet draperies, the gleam of the piano in the corner, the thick rose-and-ivory Oriental carpet all made for a setting of an old-fashioned romance. Not, Bree knew, that Simon would notice.

He'd started the fire to check out the chimney, the lights were dim to save on electricity, and his sole interest in the chess game was to whale the tar out of her.

Hunched over the board, his face caught the reflection from the ruby-globed lamp. The strong bones and deep-set eyes had the same carved intentness of the white marble chess king. He cautiously moved a pawn.

She zipped her bishop across the board, a choice that made him look at her with grave pity and methodically roll up his shirtsleeves. "You'd better take a sip of that sherry," he advised. "This is going to hurt."

"So you say." Bree chuckled. Normally she could beat him. Simon was ten times the superior player, but he became paralyzed when she made impulsive, sweeping moves. He always assumed she had a strategic reason that required defensive analysis. She never did. She played for the sheer love of the game, but tonight she was distracted, her mood wistful and restive.

They'd had a good time—a wonderful time—that afternoon, but Simon had closed up on the way home. Bree knew why. He'd almost kissed her on that grassy butte. He'd been leaning over her, his sun-warmed hand on her cheek, his eyes as deep and dark as they were right now...and then Jessica had come bound-

ing over the rise. Simon had closed up tighter than the
lid on a jar and stayed that way.

An almost kiss was like almost winning an election,
she kept telling herself. What never happened was
worth tiddledywinks. Except that it had been Simon
who had almost kissed her, not her sleepwalker, and
the fine, dry air on that butte had been volatilely electric. For a man who believed he lacked passion, he'd
sent out a nuclear-powerful charge. She wanted to
know how that kiss might have gone...yet didn't. She
wanted to know what Simon had felt at that moment . . . yet was afraid to know.

Take a belt of that sherry and let it alone, Reynaud, she told herself.

"Did you end up reaching your parents after dinner?"

There now. A reasonably safe conversational topic
to pursue. "Not my mother. Apparently my parents
were out to dinner, but I hooked up with Stephan—my
oldest brother." As Simon was aware, she called her
family twice a week. They would have worried if she
didn't. "The whole clan's fine."

"They want you home?"

"Families have a habit of wanting to herd up their
stray lambs," she said wryly.

"And are you going home after you leave here?"

The question was casual—Simon's gaze was fixed
on the board—but it put a new knot in her stomach.
In a few more days, the work crew would be done. A
few days after that, Liz would pick up Jessica. And
then Bree would run out of excuses to stay in South
Dakota . . . and anywhere near Simon.

"You're not paying attention," he scolded. "You don't want to move your rook there, honey. You leave your queen completely unprotected."

"You forget she's the toughest piece on the board, *cher*. She can take care of herself."

"You think so?" He moved a knight, then angled forward to refill her sherry glass from a decanter on the Bombay chest. "You have a habit of taking daredevil risks with your queen," he warned her.

"As I conceive the game, that's her job. To take risks. Chess is set up with the king as the most vulnerable player and the queen the most powerful. It's her job to use that strength to do whatever she has to do to protect him."

"In concept, that's true. In reality, she needs to carefully choose which risks she takes, because if the king loses his queen, the game is almost always lost. She needs to take very good care of herself. She needs to be cautious." Simon took a sip of the cognac at his side. "You didn't answer my question."

"What question?" Why did she suddenly have the confusing feeling that Simon hadn't been talking about kings and queens in a chess game?

"I asked if you were going home to your family."

She shook her head. "I'm lonesome for them—I love them all—but home isn't southern Louisiana anymore. Not for me."

He said quietly, "You're tired of traveling, Bree."

A log fell, sending a shower of sparks up the chimney. She fell silent as they continued to play, but not for long. His comment had been an invitation to talk—not chitchat conversation, but communication. It wasn't the first time he'd offered to listen, but it was the first time Bree thought the doors of communication might open both ways. If she took the risk.

She curled her knees under her and bent over the chessboard. "I've had three," she mentioned casually.

"Three what?"

"Three lovers. Although I'm not sure you could more than technically classify the first two in that category. There was a redhead when I was sixteen—a one-shot experience in sheer stupidity. He was from the wrong side of the tracks, and I felt sorry for him. About four years later there was a premed student. Mr. Medicine added up to more of an emotional commitment, but it was only one shot in the sack with him, too. He needed someone. I thought I was that someone."

Her tone had never been breezier, and her head never lifted from the chessboard.

"And about two years after that, I fell for the C.E.O. of the company I worked for, and I have to admit I fell hard. I thought we were headed for rings and prenuptial agreements and a time-shared condo and maybe even kids. As it happens, Matthew was still seeing his ex-wife. I didn't even know she was in the wings. He had to be one tired puppy, because he managed to get her pregnant at the same time he was—"

Simon said a succinct four-letter word. "Honey, I would never have asked you—"

"Play chess, Courtland." She still hadn't looked up, didn't want to look up, didn't want to know what his expression looked like. "I know you wouldn't have asked me. This was strictly a volunteer situation.

You're right, I'm tired of traveling. And as you guessed before, wanderlust wasn't the only reason I went on the road. It wasn't the men, either. It was me. Everybody's a fool once, but a second time is not so excusable, and three strikes is an out in anybody's ball game. I was making a pattern of mistakes. I wanted to break that pattern."

"Bree—"

She'd never seen Simon lose focus on the game. Her queen was free to tear right down the board. "I think I was hoping that if I confessed my past, you might feel free to unload, too."

"Unload?"

Bree said softly, "I don't think you talk to anyone. Not about what matters to you. Everyone who calls is handing you a problem. You listen, you handle, you take care of, you fix things, but you don't talk, Courtland. When do you ever get the chance to unload? About things like how you felt about your father, or if you felt shafted and angry after your divorce, or about needs and dreams and things you're afraid of. It's no wonder you sleepwalk—"

"Reynaud."

"What?"

"You took my knight."

"Yes."

"You took my knight!"

"Yes. Check your king. I believe you'll find he's cornered," Bree murmured.

But she was wrong. She got a kiss across the board—a fast smack like a brother would buss a sister who just bested him—but the diversion of the stupid game ended the evening. She may have cornered the white marble king, but the flesh-and-blood man was trickier. Simon toasted her sherry with his cognac, but the conversation was lost. Within fifteen minutes, the chess pieces were repacked in their box, he'd wished her a good-night and disappeared up the stairs.

Probably couldn't wait to get away from the nosy, busybody Gypsy, Bree thought morosely.

Since there was no chance of her sleeping, she poured another glass of sherry and fetched a book from the den. Walking back to the parlor, she told herself that Simon's fast retreat was a good omen. If he'd opened up, really talked with her, her feelings for him would only have deepened.

Every time she was near him, she felt a kick in her pulse. Part of that kick was good, healthy lust—a predictable reaction for a man she loved—but part of that kick had a stomach-dropping, trembly dimension to it. She was afraid. Admitting her draw to Simon was different than admitting a draw to her sleepwalker. The flesh-and-blood man was more alluring, more fascinating and much more dangerous.

Crouching by the hearth, she threw another log on the fire and for a moment watched the mesmerizing flames lap around their new prey. It was how she had felt in her past relationships—like prey. A man needed her. She willingly opened her heart. He took what she had and left dust in his wake.

Fear of repeating the old pattern shook her, and it seemed so much the same. Simon had needed some help. She'd given it…and day by day, living with him, she'd seen the rewarding metamorphosis of a man coming into his own, changing, beginning to reach out to the things that mattered to him again. And she'd fallen in love, exactly like that old nasty pattern again—only it wasn't. She'd fallen in love before, but not like this. Not so hard, never this deeply, never with this complex interweaving of emotion for a soul mate, a man who touched her at so many levels. . . .

The stakes have gone that high, Reynaud?

Yes.

He talked about your leaving. Does that sound like a man who wants a future with you?

No.

Don't do it, chère. Don't get any more involved. This isn't about being foolish—it's about losing your whole damn heart. Get smart, get scared, get tough.

Turning away from the fire, she forced herself to stretch out on the carpet with the book and her sherry. She opened the book to page one and belatedly discovered that she'd picked up one of Uncle Fee's—a comprehensive text on the geology of the Badlands.

If it couldn't bore her into relaxing, nothing could.

Minutes passed, then a half hour, then an hour. The chime clock sonorously ticked in the hall. Shadows darkened. A log occasionally popped in the fire, and the hot bed of coals sizzled red. The book wasn't as tedious as she thought, not once she forced herself to concentrate.

She turned another page, reached for the glass of sherry and felt a trickle of awareness sneak up her spine. Her head jerked toward the doorway, and she felt a dozen needle-sharp nerves twist in her stomach. She thought, No, please, Simon. You wouldn't do this to me tonight. I just can't handle this tonight. . . . Don't do this to me.

But Simon was already walking toward her. Not the button-down Simon she'd played chess with, but her bare-chested, dark-eyed, so alluring midnight caller.

"Simon, go back to bed," Bree said desperately.

Simon didn't. He came toward her. The book fell from her lap as she twisted to her feet. The fire caught in her hair, shot it with light. She was wearing the same red loose-necked T-shirt and white jeans she'd played chess in. And her eyes were as dark as wet coals.

She stood there as still as a frozen fawn and then seemed to shake herself a little. She took a firm step toward him with one arm outstretched. "Simon, you're sleepwalking. It's okay. I'll take you to bed—"

So that's how she talked to him, he thought. Soothingly, meltingly softly, lovingly. She hooked an arm around his waist, obviously intending to lead him toward the stairs.

She wasn't prepared when he framed her face between his palms and kissed her. She tasted like sherry, but beneath that flavor was something sweeter, darker, uniquely Bree. It was one of the things that had driven him crazy—whether he'd remember kissing her, remember what she tasted like.

Simon remembered nothing, but he hadn't been able to sleep, thinking about those eyes. Thinking about a woman who gave and gave and gave. Thinking about those three turkeys who'd used her.

When he'd walked downstairs, he hadn't really intended to go through with this, to pretend he was sleepwalking—the idea was half-brained and cowardly. It lacked honor and honesty. It was wrong.

Only there seemed no other way. He couldn't let her go on believing every man was like those three jerks. To never give back anything for all she'd given him was equally unlivable. He wanted to make Bree feel loved and special . . . only he was rotten with words, rotten with expressing emotion.

Excuses, Courtland, he thought.

Yes. But they didn't seem so indefensible now. Bree's mouth was mobile under his—mobile and trembly and fragile. Her lips knew his. Her fingers clenched his shoulders, hard, as if she were fighting to stay in control, and the last thing in hell Simon wanted was to force anything on her—even a kiss. But then her lashes shuttered down and her face tilted and her arms climbed, then coiled around his neck.

Emotion poured from her. Hunger. Fear. A wistful, wistful yearning and a hold-me kind of longing. And Simon felt the bittersweet awareness that he'd been right, not wrong. She felt a freedom with her sleepwalker that she'd never have felt with him. She wanted the fantasy, not him, and inadequacy gnawed at his nerve. He was good at self-discipline and control—there was no way he'd let this go too far—but impossibly inexperienced at fathoming a woman's heart.

Simon Courtland was no woman's fantasy.

He didn't even know how to try.

Slowly, though, he discovered one of those elemental truths unique to loving someone. He wasn't alone. Bree . . . was going to help him. Tongues touched, dry at first, then wooing warm, then wet. She made a soft sound, a keening sound when he dragged her closer.

So, he thought, not too gentle. She liked feeling a little taken over, taken under.

He claimed her mouth again, then trailed a ring of kisses on her jaw, her cheek, her brow. They were reverent, cherishing kisses, the kisses of a lover aggressively seeking her pleasure. She liked those, too. He knew because she swayed closer and she clung, length to length, as if he were her last ballast and only buoy. As if she needed him. As if she wanted him. Even . . . as if she loved him.

He lifted his head, breathing harder than a shaky freight train, damningly aware that his whole body was hot and aching. The control he'd counted on was not so absolute. Bree had lifted her head, too, but her eyes stayed closed and her voice was barely a thread. "Simon, I'm afraid."

He kissed her again. Hard and fiercely. He'd have shot himself before hurting Bree or doing anything to scare her. How could she not know?

"Simon—you've done this before. Come to me, as if you knew what I wanted, knew what I needed, only tonight . . . I don't want to know what's in my mind tonight, *cher*. Because I don't think I'm strong enough to stop you, and I'm not sure this is what you want. . . ."

He folded her close, his heart slamming so hard that he couldn't breathe. At that moment he'd have given a year of his life to know what she'd wanted those other nights. To know what he'd done. Because her voice sure as hell wasn't breaking for the Simon Courtland she'd had breakfast with.

His big hands splayed, stroking her throat, then her collarbone, then her slim shoulders. She was trem-

bling, and Simon meant the caresses to soothe her.
They didn't. She was looking at him, waiting, shivery, tense. The last log dropped in the fireplace,
creating a shower of sparks, and the fire made a
shadow on the far wall...a silhouette of the two of
them, locked like lovers in the silence of the room.

The silhouette changed when he slowly pulled off
her T-shirt. He warned himself that the boundaries of
fantasy and reality were becoming blurred, but it
wasn't that simple. Her long hair crackled with electricity, then cascaded down her back when she lifted
her face to his. She wore nothing beneath the T. From
her throat to the waistband of her jeans, her skin was
a pure porcelain pearl, flushed from the fire and desire, and there was a yearning in her face...a yearning that Simon hadn't expected to inspire in any
woman, and certainly never Bree.

Yet his so passionate and earthy Bree suddenly
turned shy. She moved to cover herself, but he caught
her wrists and looked his fill, then slowly raised his
eyes to meet hers. She was precious. She was beautiful. He kissed her so she knew. He kissed her as he'd
kissed no other woman, and years poured into that
embrace, thirty-five years of never knowing this slow,
dark fire of emotion even existed. He kissed her until
her lips were red and wet and her eyes were a pure liquid blue, a dazed blue.

"Simon...you don't know what you're doing to me.
You weren't...like this before. I never..."

It came to him like a surprise. The pulse and purr of
a man's power, a lover's power to tempt and please,
excite and love. He wasn't Simon at that moment. He
was nothing more, nothing less than a man. Her man.

And when he reached for the snap on her jeans, her throat made another of those sounds. A wild, raw woman's sound, a call of need, and her eyes locked on his.

She wanted this. She wanted him.

The zipper went down. His palms slid inside the jeans to push them off, and she bucked toward him, blindly, helplessly. She reached for his head to pull his mouth down, and he could feel her fingers on his scalp, feel the passion coiling like an electric current all through her.

A wisp of blue silk came off with her jeans, and by then he'd lowered her to the thick patch of carpet by the fire. Naked, her skin was fire-lit and softer than satin, far too soft for a bed of scratchy carpet, but just then, she didn't seem to notice.

His head ducked to her breasts. He buffed her nipples with his tongue as his palm dipped lower, lower, until he discovered the juncture between her thighs. He cupped her there. Released her. When he tried it again, her legs clamped around him and she bit his shoulder. Hard.

She shouldn't have, because he suddenly had another clue about what she liked . . . and what he could give her, as a man, as a lover. His loins felt on fire. He ignored his own need. His muscles were all taut, his skin fevered. He ignored that, too. This was for Bree.

He kissed her mouth again, hard, then branded more hard kisses down her throat, stopping at her breasts. She liked a little roughness, but never near her breasts. He'd already discovered that the small white orbs were exquisitely, unbearably sensitive. He grasped a fistful of her long, silky hair and whisked the strands over the coral tips of her nipples, tickling whisks, whisper-soft whisks.

The Gypsy tried to bite him again, and her hands were getting in his way. Tenderly, firmly, Simon had to restrain her. He'd obviously found a pattern she liked, and he went with it. The rough, claiming, erotic kisses. Then the whisper whisks. Then down to cup her, lingering there longer each time, the heel of his hand rubbing while his finger invaded her soft core. Then he released her and started all over again, each time tempting her closer to climax.

He knew what she wanted.

He knew she was close.

And that was when it all went to hell.

Her hands pushed hard at his shoulders, and unprepared, he toppled back. Bree sprawled half on top of him, her hair all dark and tangled, and her eyes blazing brighter than the coals. "Not alone, *cher*. If you're going to drive me over the edge, believe me, you're going with me."

He'd never lost control with a woman, but she started salting kisses on his throat, his chest. With her hands, with her tongue, she told him that she loved his body, that she desired him. *Him*. She liked that trick with the hair; she swished those long strands down the length of him until he thought he'd burn up. She hooked her fingers in the waistband of his underwear, and somehow in the process of her trying to drag the damn briefs off him the two of them were rolling on the carpet. Close to the fire and the bright, hot lick of flame, and then away, where it was cool and dark and there was nothing but Bree. Her lips were above him, then below, with kisses that teased him, kisses that haunted him, and suddenly he knew exactly how much trouble he was in.

He pinned her beneath him, roughly, too roughly. "Bree—"

"Shh."

But the fantasy of being her phantom lover wasn't right. Lord, it was exactly what he'd wanted to be, but not now. Now he needed her to know that it was him, Simon, that he was awake, aware, that there was no game involved. "Sweetheart—"

"Shh." Her whisper was urgent, frantic. "Please, Simon. I love you, and I want this and I want you. Now. Please. Please..."

She pulled him to her with that hoarse cry of love echoing in his head, and he thought, Hell. Because he knew he'd lost it. He wrapped her legs around him and took her mouth at the same time that he drove inside her, deeply, completely.

He knew he should care whether she believed him to be Simon or a fantasy. He didn't.

Their flesh fused; her skin was as slick as salty butter. So was his. What she wanted was what he wanted. There was no difference. The fire was hot, but it was her softness that melted him, way deep on the inside. She was an uninhibited giver, loving, sweet, wild. She called his name as if she were beckoning his soul. She called it again, and then she cried it when her whole body arched in climax.

Release rocketed through him in an agony of pleasure. Even then, he knew this was no act of passion for him.

He'd given his soul to the Gypsy.

* * *

Later, when he could breathe again, when the spent weakness of desire allowed his spinning mind to function, Simon forced himself to remember the obvious.

Bree didn't necessarily want his soul.

She'd been badly hurt. She'd been vulnerable. And maybe she'd needed a lover to heal and erase old bad memories.

But that sure as hell didn't mean she was in love with Simon Courtland.

Ninc

The fire had burned to embers. Bree was still wrapped in the cocoon of Simon's arms, her cheek still nestled against his chest. Languorously, almost hypnotically, his fingers sifted through her hair. His touch was possessive and tender. Maybe he intended to soothe her.

Unfortunately, even a buffalo-size tranquilizer wasn't likely to soothe her. Reactions were setting in. Her heart was beating faster than a clattering roller coaster.

His lovemaking had taken her out. Completely. She knew Simon was lonely. She knew he had an emotional, sensual side to his nature that had been locked up for a long time.

She hadn't guessed how deep those still waters really were. He'd come alive for her, with her. He'd been passionate, demanding, a woman's fantasy of a pirate lover, a ravager of her pleasure, a thief of her inhibitions...and a giver, as Bree had never imagined a man could be a giver.

She understood the sense of wonder she'd found with him.

She was unprepared for the anxiety, building fearfast, the longer she lay in his arms. The symptoms were unmistakable. The taste of dread, the thick thudding of her heart, the overwhelming sensation of foreboding as if she'd just crossed the path of a very black cat and now came the price.

She'd done it before—loved a man who didn't love her—and she'd sworn to break that pattern, to never again lay her heart on the line that way. This time was different, but only because Simon had captured a vulnerable niche of her soul as well as her heart. The rest of the pattern was painfully familiar. He had needed someone, but that kind of need was temporary. And he desired her, but passion wasn't love.

"Bree. Honey—"

At the first sound of Simon's husky voice, she squeezed her eyes closed. Quicker than a coiled spring, she sprang loose from his warm arms and stood up. "Shh, love. I'll take you up to bed, Simon. I know it's cold and it's late. I'll take care of you."

Even to her own ears, her voice sounded tinny and strained...and silly, as if she thought she were talking to a half-conscious sleepwalker.

Simon suddenly went completely still.

With her back to him, she banked the last of the fire and folded a metal screen in front of the grate, then searched for their clothes. Rather embarrassingly, her T-shirt was gracing a lamp shade, and she seemed to have wantonly thrown his underwear behind a chair. If Simon had any doubts about his "less than passionate" nature, they'd surely buried that dead horse.

So smile for him, Reynaud, she urged herself. Only she couldn't smile right then. She picked up the clothes, aware Simon was watching her, feeling his gaze boring into her bare back as she determinedly chatted to him. "I know you never remember what happens by morning, *cher,* but I don't want you picking up any unconscious...anxiety. I've been on the Pill for four months. Not because I expected to need it. My cycle was all mixed up—probably because of so much traveling—and when I saw a doctor, he suggested a six-month run on the Pill...."

Stupid, stupid, stupid. The fake sound in her voice made her cringe on the inside, and Simon still hadn't moved. He was watching her, studying her with fathomlessly dark eyes.

She knew he was awake. She hadn't realized that the first instant he'd walked into the parlor, but very soon after. Her sleepwalker's kisses had always made her feel safe. But tonight even Simon's first kisses had obliterated any feeling of safety and come close to burning her up. As she had always guessed, he was a far more dangerous lover than his alter ego. Just before they'd made love, he'd suddenly seemed to realize that she might have her "lovers" confused. He'd stopped. He'd tried to tell her.

She hadn't let him. Then, her response had been instinctive and blind. That instinct was even more powerful now.

Bree swiveled one last glance around the room, then padded barefoot back to Simon. Her gaze fixed on his

throat, mouth, hair, shoulders—anywhere, anywhere, anywhere but his eyes. "Okay, love. The fire's
taken care of and the room is exactly as it was. There'll
be no reason in the morning for you to worry that
anything happened, *cher*. Take my hand and I'll take
you to bed."

Still, he hadn't moved and his eyes had yet to leave
her face. He didn't understand what she was doing,
but he seemed to sense how terribly distraught she was.
Please, Simon. Please go along with me....

Given time to think, he would surely realize that the
situation would be incomparably easier if they both
pretended it hadn't happened. Other lovers couldn't
do that. They could. His real sleepwalking problem
made that uniquely possible. Jekyll never remembered what Hyde had done. She was treating him as if
she believed he was sleepwalking; all he had to do was
go along, and it could be business as usual in the
morning.

Come on, Reynaud. The idea is half-baked and bizarre and stupid. But it wasn't, she told herself
fiercely. Tomorrow morning it should be business as
usual. The real world hadn't changed because they'd
made love. She was still leaving soon. Because she'd
fallen in love with him was no reason to believe he felt
the same way.

She could picture him fumbling with the awkward
emotional business of admitting he had no interest in
a permanent relationship. She'd heard it all before. If
heartache was involved, Bree knew she'd asked for it.
But dammit, Simon, you'll break my heart if you tell
me I'm nothing more than a short, sweet encounter.

It didn't have to happen. Maybe the idea was half-baked and bizarre, but it would save them both from being hurt.

"Wait, Simon. I forgot to turn out the globed lamp, and I'll turn on the hall light so we aren't stumbling upstairs in the dark."

As she hustled around handling the lights, she saw with enormous relief that Simon was lurching to his feet. Juggling their clothes under one arm, she took his hand and thought, Almost home free. He was going to let it go. All she had to do now was get him upstairs.

Only it seemed she'd counted those chickens a little too quickly.

He lifted her hand instead of taking it. "We have to go upstairs, *cher*. It's late. Terribly late...." His thumb discovered her nerves-damp palm, the shaky pulse in her wrist. As though he suddenly understood that it was fear driving her, he gently released her hand. "There's nothing for you to worry about. Nothing. By morning all you're going to remember is a good night's sleep." His knuckle nudged her chin up. His eyes swept her pale face with fierce, unfathomable intensity. And then his mouth came down on hers.

It was a hell of a way to shut her up. His kiss was so tender, so incomparably gentle that she felt the idiotic prick of tears.

And then he took her hand and led her up the stairs.

To his room.

And his bed.

"All clean." Simon folded the washrag on the side of the porcelain tub and pulled the plug.

"Good," Jessica said fervently. "I hate baths."

With a chuckle he wrapped a towel around his slippery little eel and half listened to her constant stream of chatter. She wanted him to read her a story before she went to bed. He agreed. She wanted to grow her hair as long as Bree's. He agreed. She wanted to sleep in her purple-and-green sweatshirt. He agreed. If Jess asked him for the moon right then, his answer would have been an equally distracted yes.

His naked daughter discarded the towel and darted down the hall toward her bedroom. Simon followed, well versed in little girls' bedtime rituals. It was big girls' bedtime rituals that had him befuddled.

For three nights now, he'd been living a bachelor's dream. Free sex with a passionately willing woman. No strings, no ties, no complications. Hell, by day the lady even pretended it hadn't happened. A guy didn't get it easier than that.

Assuming a guy wanted scot-free sex with no complications, the situation was ideal.

Assuming, however, that the guy wanted to sneak a ring onto the lady's finger with *all* the complications implied by commitment, the situation was damned tricky.

Simon hunched by the stack of books in Jessica's pink bedroom, sorting through for her favorites. His hand landed, with some irony, on *A Nightmare in My Closet*.

Sleepwalking had always been his nightmare, but never quite like this. He'd already considered the obvious—that Bree was using his problem to let him down easy. She wanted the fantasy, not the real man. She was willing to have an affair, but she didn't want commitment. After all, why should she? He was a man who had a lot to learn about expressing emotion. A man who had shut himself off for so long that he had miles to learn about what a woman needed in a loving relationship.

"Daddy?"

It wasn't that Simon wasn't perfectly willing to bog down into an abyss of masculine insecurities. But every time he methodically considered the problem, he knew something more was wrong. Each time he tried to talk with her, she got this look in her eyes. This fragile, crushable, panicked "don't" look.

So she was scared. Which Simon could understand. Too damn many men had told her they cared—and lied. Bree was a little high-strung, a little volatile, on the subject of trust.

"Daddy."

He had briefly mulled the idea of sitting on Bree's chest and spooning cognac down her throat until she talked about it. But that was no good. Although it went against his sense of honor and ethics to keep up the sleepwalking pretense, at some intrinsic level he understood that trust was never won with talk.

If he was to win Bree's trust, he had to do it with action. He had to show her that he was changing, too. Growing, with her. Maybe he'd been a little corny, bringing her wildflowers two nights ago. Maybe he'd gone a little too far last night with the baby oil.

But it seemed he was making headway. Instinctively he sensed that his strongest weapon was their nights, because in the dark, all the chips went down. In the dark, Bree was her most vulnerable, her most defenseless...and her most honest. Each night had been a burning, unforgettable explosion of desire and emotion. How could she possibly give herself to him so completely if she didn't love him? She put her soul on the line.

And so did he.

He couldn't lose that Gypsy. He didn't want to corral her, rope her down, quench her free spirit. He just wanted to love her and protect all that was fragile and special in Bree. She was the best thing that had ever happened to him. He couldn't let her go. More time, Simon kept telling himself. He just needed more time....

A pillow thwacked the back of his head, nearly throwing him off balance. Startled, he pivoted on his heel, only to get another pillow full in the face. "Daddy! I've had it with you! You weren't listening to a word I said!"

His urchin—the one jumping on top of the mattress in an insane purple-and-green sweatshirt—was right. He hadn't been listening. It was because of Bree that he had a new conception of loving his daughter. Love—the right kind of love—was always serious. Yet when you spent love, you had more. And a sense of lightness and laughter sealed the edges on that gift.

He slowly stood up and, stern faced, lifted one of the pillows. Pedantic as a judge, he began a lecture. "It's a bad idea to throw pillows. Very bad."

Something in his expression must have tipped her off, because her eyes were dancing. "Oh, yeah?"

"Oh, yeah, precisely. Roughhousing and wild play inevitably end up in trouble. I'm afraid you need a critical lesson in judgment, Jess. Very critical."

When he gently plopped the pillow on her head, she erupted into giggles.

Bree, coming fresh from the downstairs shower a few minutes later, heard the incredible noise coming from upstairs—screams and howls and banshee cries. With a towel wrapped around her head turban-style, she took the stairs two at a time and flew down the hall.

She stopped dead in the doorway to Jessica's bedroom. Feathers, thicker than snow, floated through the entire room. Lamp shades were topsy-turvy, bedclothes hurled, toys and books sprawled. Jess was crouched on one side of the bed, Simon had ducked down on the other, and both of them were laughing side-splitting hard. Her heart swelled. She couldn't help it. Simon still had a pinch of child left in him, but Bree never thought he'd find it . . . never thought he'd let it go. *Courtland, you can't imagine how much I love you.*

The moment was clearly a bond for father and daughter. Bree didn't want to intrude. She'd have tiptoed out of sight, only it was too late for escape. Two pairs of eyes, both deep-set charcoal gray, both guilty as hell, spotted her at the same time.

"Uh-oh," Jessica said with a gulp, and to her dad, "I think you're gonna get it, Daddy."

Bree propped her hands on her hips and adopted the most furious expression she knew. "This is appalling. This is disgraceful. Do either of you realize how long this is going to take to clean up? I have *never* seen such a mess—"

A pillow soared through the air, showering flakes of feathers in its wake, and landed splat on her face.

It had been thrown, without question, by the six-foot-two devil on the far side of the bed.

At eleven at night, the six-foot-two devil reappeared at the far side of her bed in the tower room. Half praying he wouldn't come, half knowing he would, Bree had dressed for bed in bra, underpants and a full-length nightgown that buttoned to the throat.

There were no feathers, no lights, no boisterous laughter in her dark bedroom, although, too late, she discovered he'd brought a toy. She heard him plunk something down on the table but didn't realize it was a tape player until he switched it on.

He caught at her hands and pulled her out of bed before she recognized the music. When she did, she felt a sinking feeling, as if she were skidding on ice and knew she was going to fall. He played it low, not loud, but the earthy, sensual beat was unmistakably from the soundtrack of *Dirty Dancing*.

He hooked her arms around his neck and laid her against him. She was stiff at first, resisting, but she'd tried that before. It never worked. Not with Simon. He moved with her in the darkness, half dancing, half making love to the pulse and sensual rhythm of the music. She'd dreamed it. She'd dreamed of dancing just like this, not with her sleepwalker, not with the formal Courtland, but with the blend of both. The man who could be.

In time, her long nightgown graced the floor. Her bra and underpants suffered the same fate. And still they danced, naked now, teasing each other, exciting each other until neither could stand it.

Bree clung fiercely, desperately when he laid her on
the bed. Every sound and texture in the darkness had
his name. His long limbs, sleek with sweat, heavy with
the scent of passion, the drugging taste of him—it
wasn't as if she could ever forget. He rode her, her
phantom lover, wickedly hard, lovingly well, tempting her beyond all reason.

She tipped over the edge, yielding for him, with
him. Moments later, though, lying trembling and sated
in his arms, she felt him stroke her cheek, heard his
husky whisper. "Bree—"

At some point, each night, he always tried it. Each
night her response was the same. "Shh," she murmured, and kissed him. If she could not deny him her
bed, she'd asked nothing of him but this. No words,
no promises of love allowed.

Tonight, especially, it hurt. She had never wanted to
be less than honest with Simon and knew he didn't
understand—but he wasn't living with her past. The
one common pattern in her old mistakes had been her
failure to face the truth. Every time, every damn time,
she'd confused need for love.

In front of her eyes, Simon was rediscovering
laughter, life, passion. Ironically, that was what shook
her the most. The more exquisite their nights, the more
painful the truth. Any day now, any night, Simon
would realize what she already knew. The more he
changed, the less he needed her.

"You're sure I'm going to look beautiful?"

"Very sure, assuming you can manage to stop
twisting around." It was hard for Bree to talk with the
edge of a comb between her teeth. It was even harder

to French braid Jessica's hair outside on a wild, windy afternoon. Kneeling on the front porch, Bree dipped the comb in the water glass, wet the hair and started winding the intricate braid again.

"Exactly how long does it take to get beautiful?"

"That's a question women have been asking since the beginning of time, *chère,* but in your case, not long."

"Sure seems like forever," Jessica said disgustedly.

Bree didn't dare chuckle. She'd have dropped the comb. French braiding a four-year-old's flyaway hair was an act of love if ever there was one. She wet and wound and wrapped until her fingers ached, but it was a savoring ache.

This morning she'd saved a growling Simon when his computer screen went blank. He was so brilliant with a complex engineering problem, so pitiful when he punched a wrong button. "You swore," he told her balefully, "you swore when I first met you that you knew nothing about business." She'd grinned at him.

Another savoring ache. Bree was storing them up, every moment, every memory, every picture. Despair would come later, as inevitable as payday, but she refused to give in to it now. She had too little time left with them. She didn't think about leaving; she just thought about savoring every minute she had, and this afternoon was a capsule of a memory in itself.

Hurly-burly clouds streaked across a cyan sky. The sun was razor hot, then chill, and there was a wild, electric taste to the air. A storm was coming, but it wasn't here yet. Tufts of wind rippled through the range grass that seemed to be growing taller and greener by the day. Eroded hills in the distance were streaked with bronze and cinnamon. So much space. So much freedom. Space for a soul to breathe, freedom for a woman to reach and work and grow in her own way.

How are you ever going to leave here, Reynaud? How are you going to leave him? She sighed. Her thoughts had no easy answers.

"Look, Bree, I've been about as good as I can get. I have to have been sitting here about four million zillion hours. Aren't you almost done?"

"Hey, is this the same kid who begged—no, groveled—to have me do this?" *How are you ever going to leave her?* "Give me sixty more seconds, *chère*. Honest, I'm working as fast as I can."

"Oh, no."

"Oh, no, what?"

"Oh, no. That's my *mom*. She's come to get me, Bree."

Bree snapped the tiny rubber band at the end of Jessica's braid and stood up. She saw the white station wagon pulling up but was sure Jess was wrong. "It can't be your mom, silly. She isn't due for days yet. And she didn't call. Even if she came back from her vacation early, she'd have called...."

Her voice trailed off. A lump filled her throat as big as a rock when the tall blonde climbed out of the car. *Not yet. Please, Liz. I just want a few more days. You can't be here yet.*

But the identity of the woman was hard to mistake when she called out, "Punkin!" For two dreadful seconds Jess, beside Bree, seemed torn with anxiety, but then the little one whipped down the porch steps to be immediately enveloped in her mother's hug.

Abruptly Bree felt windblown, untucked and too damned short—Liz was almost as tall as Simon, regal and statuesque in build. She was wearing a cream shirt and tan jeans, both a little travel wrinkled, but the casual clothes fit exactly right. Old money, Bree thought dourly. Maybe Liz didn't have it, but she looked it. Poise, classic features, grace. In no crisis in your life, Reynaud, have you ever been wearing shoes.

It was several moments before Liz looked up and spotted her.

"Mommy, this is *Bree*."

"So I guessed." Liz walked toward her, extending a hand. "Simon told me about you when I called. It's nice to meet you."

Neither the poise nor the classic grace could conceal a wet palm or shaky fingers. Liz was nervous, shook-up. Close up, Bree saw the fine lines of strain, the mobile mouth trying too hard to smile.

That quick, Bree guessed who was going to be stuck taking charge, and it didn't matter who was barefoot. *Can't anything be simple in this life?* By no stretch of the imagination had she ever fathomed warming up to Liz. Because of Jess, Bree had automatically given Simon's ex-wife brownie points as a mother, but her heart's loyalty was to Simon. Liz had needed Simon, used him, jettisoned him. Bree had entertained more than one satisfyingly violent daydream about taking the lady out.

Only it wasn't going to work that way. This was no cold-blooded user, but a five-foot-eleven waif. Bree knew precisely what Liz's arrival meant—a last-minute countdown on her own time with Simon and Jess—but she could hardly take out her troubles on a woman with her own. "Come on inside," Bree welcomed her, and backed up to the door. "I'll find Simon for you."

"He may be . . . irritated. I should have called—"

"He won't be irritated," Bree said firmly.

"I won't be in your way that long—"

Caretaker fashion, Bree herded her charges inside. "You're not in anyone's way. We're all thrilled to see you. The wind's wild enough to work up a thirst, isn't it? I'll get you some iced tea."

Simon must have heard the commotion in the front hall, because he strode from the direction of the office with a perplexed frown. "Bree?" He paused midstride when he recognized his ex-wife.

Liz so carefully straightened her shoulders. "Hello, Simon."

"Liz."

"I cut my vacation short. I couldn't stand it any longer without seeing Jess, and I thought we'd better talk about the situation."

"It's past time," Simon agreed, and looked at Bree.

She had the craziest sensation that he wanted to spirit her off and leave his ex-wife standing in the hall. Something was going on here that she didn't understand, but there was no time to dwell on it. "How about if I get you all something to drink, and I'm sure Jess is dying to show her mom the house. Maybe after that, you two could catch a few private minutes while Jessica and I fool around in the kitchen."

A half hour later, Bree had Jessica standing on a chair in the kitchen, shredding lettuce at the sink. It was a favorite job for the little one, leaving Bree with a dinner menu to plan around a fresh salad. Breaded

veal *panne* and pasta? Was there time to whip up a
Cajun satsuma cake? Was there an etiquette book
somewhere about what you were supposed to feed an
ex-wife?

She glanced down, well aware of how quiet Jessica
was, how fast her little fingers were tearing up the lettuce leaves. Poor baby, she was so tense. She pushed
her blue-rimmed glasses back on her nose, leaving a
thumbprint smudge on the lens, and kept glancing at
the door. Jess knew her parents were talking, knew
that her mother had come to take her back.

Bree squeezed her shoulders, but there was nothing
she could say. She, too, knew that Liz had come to
take her back.

The afternoon had become so cloudy that the
kitchen turned gloomy and dark. Bree had just
switched on the overhead light when Liz walked in, her
face as pale as ash. She immediately walked over to
Jessica and hooked her arms around her. "Hey, punkin. Your daddy's been telling me what a good time
you've been having. You like it here?"

"I *love* it here, Mom."

Liz smiled, but Bree could see the woman's pain in
it. "Daddy thinks you might like to stay with him."

"Yes!"

"And that's fine," Liz said gaily. "If you want to,
you can spend more time with Daddy. For now. Not
forever, but for now. Okay, lovebug?"

It should have been exactly what Jess wanted to
hear, yet for a snapshot second the little one looked
desperately at Bree. She saw, but at that precise instant, she was feeling stunned. That's why they talked
so long. Simon was fighting for his daughter. And he'd

wanted to tell her. That's what that look in the front hall had been about.

"If you think it's easy for me to leave her, you're wrong."

Belatedly Bree realized that Jess had flown from the kitchen and she was alone with Simon's ex-wife. "Liz, I never doubted that you love Jess," she said awkwardly.

Liz was staring out the window with hard, dry eyes. "She always had this kindred spirit thing with Simon. When she was a baby, all it took was Simon to walk into a room and she'd quit crying. And about six months ago, she woke me in the middle of the night to call him. He'd been in a car accident. He wasn't hurt, but it was as if she knew. And a few weeks ago, when she got it in her head that she wanted to be with Simon..." Liz shook her head. "I never knew what I was supposed to do. How can a four-year-old be so headstrong? And if she really wants to live with her father instead of me..."

"If you're feeling guilty, I think there's no need for it," Bree said quietly. "When I was a kid, I can remember a million times when I turned to my dad. And another million when I needed my mom. Maybe Jess is at a time in her life when she needs Simon, but that doesn't mean she loves you any less."

Liz wrapped her arms around her chest. "You think so?"

"I know so."

"I worry so much that it's something I'm doing wrong. That I'm somehow failing her as a mother."

"Good grief, Liz. Step back and take a good look. She's a bright, wonderful, mischievous, healthy, creative child with a heart as big as the sky. You call that failing?''

"Bree.'' There was a different expression in her eyes now.

"What?''

"It's not hard to understand why my daughter thinks you're something special.'' Absently Liz lifted a pot lid on the stove. "Simon, too. I don't know what you've done with Simon, but he's a completely different man.''

"Different?''

"I've never talked with him like we did this afternoon. We usually cover our business, then he asks me if I need any money, and it's all done. Strangers could have the same conversation.''

Bree didn't know what to say.

"It wasn't much different when we were married,'' Liz admitted. "He was good to me. Considerate, always. When I first met him, I fell head over heels. He was good-looking and assured—he'd done so much with his life, even that young—and there was nothing he couldn't handle. I'd never met anyone that strong. I knew he was quiet, but over time I thought that would change, that he would open up to me.'' She shook her head. "I never touched him. Not in any way that mattered. You have.''

"Liz—''

"Yes, I know. This is an awkward conversation, not exactly what you'd expect to hear from an ex-wife. But I'm in a position to know more than anyone...that he needs you.'' Liz smiled and then dropped the conversation. "It looks like a storm's coming. If I'm going

to hit the road, I'd better do it, but I want to see Jess
a few more minutes before I go.''

Left alone, Bree abruptly started moving around the
kitchen. Fast. She diced anything she could find to
finish the salad, started the water for pasta, pounded
and breaded enough of her veal *panne* for an army. No
matter how hard she worked, Liz's words kept pop-
ping into her mind. *I never touched him. You have. He
needs you.*

Outside, black-bellied clouds cuddled lower on the
horizon, but so far there wasn't a spit of rain. The
brightly lighted kitchen started to fill up with familiar
messes and wonderful smells, yet Bree felt agitated and
upset. She wanted to believe Liz's words. Too damn
much. Only there was no phrase on earth that had
gotten her in more trouble than *wanted to.*

The truth was right in front of her eyes. Simon was
fine now. During the past few weeks, he had relooked
at what mattered to him and was changing in wonderfully healthy directions. Their nights were one example. His laughter during the day was another. And
today he'd fought for time with Jess—yet another sign
that his priorities had changed, that he was reaching
out for what was important to him.

*Simon doesn't need you, Reynaud. Not for any-
thing. Not anymore.*

Until Bree glanced up from the stove, she didn't realize he was standing in the doorway. The look of him
only underlined the thoughts in her mind. Simon really
had changed. When she'd first met him, his eyes were
as hard as a mirror, self-discipline dominating the way
he walked, talked, moved.

The hardness was gone, replaced by a different kind of strength. He was alive again, vital, sexy, full of energy and a new determination of purpose that showed in his face. As he walked toward her, he looked ready to move mountains.

At that precise moment, it never occurred to her that she was the mountain he intended to move.

"Liz is gone?" she asked.

"She's been gone. I've been standing here for ten minutes, watching you fly around the kitchen. Are we feeding the marines?" he asked humorously.

"I may have overdone the quantities a little—" She sucked in her breath when his hands closed on her shoulders. Unfortunately he knew her body better than she did. Automatically, instinctively, he discovered the taut, strained muscles at the back of her neck.

"You're beat. Which you should be. You've been taking care of people all day. Me, Jess, and from what I understand, you gave Liz a dose of TLC, as well." He swept aside her hair so he could attack her tired muscles more freely. "We need to have a little talk, Reynaud."

"Talk?" He was making it impossible for her to think. His voice was husky and low and scraped her nerves like all those promises she wanted to believe in.

"You're very good at taking care of people. Very bad at talking. You once gave me a lecture about that, but somewhere along the way you forgot to take your own medicine."

"Simon—"

"After dinner, once Jessica is asleep, we're going to talk. About you and what you want. I'll bring the wine up to the tower room. We've communicated damn well there, Bree. And if it takes the whole bottle of wine, you're going to tell me what you're afraid of."

Her heart thrummed erratically. We've communicated damn well there, Bree. The game was up, the pretense over. She should have known he wouldn't let it go on forever, and she wasn't sure if she felt more relief . . . or fear.

Suddenly, her fingertips chilled and a ghost shiver tingled down her spine. She did feel fear—not for the coming talk with Simon, but fear like a knot of anxiety, premonitory, consuming. "Simon, where's Jessica?"

His hands tightened on her shoulders, and his tone was edged with impatience. "She was upstairs with her mother until Liz left. I assume she still is. Dammit, don't do this, Bree. I've let it go because I thought you needed time, needed to learn that you could trust me. But it's gone too far. We are going to talk, no evasions and no excuses."

Bree turned in his arms. She couldn't get it out of her head—that brief, desperate look in Jess's eyes when the child had been talking with Liz. "I think we should look for her."

"Why?" he demanded.

It wasn't a good answer, but it was all she had. "Because something feels wrong."

She saw Simon's eyes shutter, his whole body go still. She'd hurt him. He thought she was shutting him out. He thought she was running away from honesty. From him. "It's not an excuse," she said urgently. "Please, Simon. Look."

Simon catered to her, but he was unwilling—at first. It didn't take either of them long to realize that Jessica wasn't upstairs. Or on the third floor. Or anywhere in the house.

By the time they both met up in the front hall, sheets of rain were starting to slash at the windows. The lights flickered when the first bolt of lightning streaked the sky. Bree remembered far too well how fast a storm could overtake this country. Complete darkness could fall in the blink of an eye. Washouts and flash floods could happen in minutes.

There was no safe place in the Badlands, not for a little girl alone in a storm.

Ten

"There's no reason to overreact, Bree. She hasn't been gone more than ten minutes, and there's only one place she'd go." Simon pulled on a yellow slicker, stuffed the pocket with a high-beam flashlight and grabbed a blanket.

"Her hideout." Bree was freely handwringing. "Simon, I just don't understand. All she wanted was to stay with you. That's exactly what happened, so this makes no sense. Why would she run off?"

"I don't know, but we'll find out. With the car, it won't take me more than a few minutes to get there and back."

"I want to go with you—"

"No," he said calmly. "She could have wandered outside for a few minutes, gotten caught in the rain and already be on her way back. If one of us wasn't here, she'd be coming into an empty house."

"But what if she didn't head for that hideout? What if—"

"Bree." Simon's palms framed her face, holding her absolutely still. His eyes were as black as wet stones and luminous with emotion. "If she's lost, I'll find her. If you were lost, I'd find you. There's nothing complicated about this. It really is that simple."

When he was gone, Bree turned off her burned dinner, collected more blankets in the front hall than a battalion of lost waifs could need and switched on all the downstairs lights. That took four minutes.

That left nothing to do but pace. Outside, the temperature started dropping and the storm was getting worse. A merciless, keening wind sneaked into every crack of the old house, and the rain beat like noisy metal needles on the windows. In twenty minutes, he still wasn't back. Twenty minutes became thirty. Then forty-five.

Simon had been predictably calm, cool and sure in a crisis. He said he'd find her. Bree knew he would. He said he'd find you, too, Reynaud. She hugged her arms to her chest, still remembering the dark, luminous look in his eyes. She'd seen the look before and assumed it was passion. Powerful, strong passion, but still passion. That moment in that hall, though, desire had been the last thing on his mind, or hers.

The look in his eyes had been remarkably, wonderfully, dangerously like...love. Real love, and the talk he'd started in the kitchen had been equally disturbing. *What if you've been wrong, Bree? What if—*

There was no time to think. Car lights reflected in the front parlor windows. She flew to the front door. Sheets of cold silver rain ran off Simon's slicker as he bent inside the car and emerged with a blanket-wrapped package. "Is she all right?" Bree called out.

"A little wet and a little hungry, but definitely fine." His hair was soaked to the scalp, rain dripping from his eyelashes as he carried Jess inside.

Bree peeled down the blanket to see the little one with the woebegone eyes and dirt-smudged cheeks and an extremely tangled French braid. "I broke my glasses, Bree." The voice was wobbly.

Maybe there was a little wobble in Bree's voice, too. "Glasses fix, *chère*. The only thing that matters is that you're okay." As soon as Simon shed his slicker, he hunkered down next to Bree. Both pairs of hands stripped Jess of her wet clothes. She was chilled, but a bath was unsafe during the lightning storm. Simon carried her upstairs and threaded on a nightgown. Bree wrapped her in a blanket, and then Simon scooped her up.

They all ended up in the kitchen. Jessica ate what was salvaged from dinner from the voluminous folds of a blanket on her father's lap. Bree fixed a plate for Simon, brought him a dry sweatshirt and towel, and because he still looked damp at the edges, poured him a straight shot of whiskey. Then, to give her two a little space, she faced the kitchen. Somehow during the past two hours, it had turned into a disaster of epic proportions.

"Mom said I could stay for now. 'For now,' Daddy. You know what that means."

"No, sweetheart. You'll have to tell me."

"It means I couldn't live with you. 'Now' never means for very long. Like if I'm riding my bike, she says 'for now.' That means I have to stop as soon as it's dinnertime." Jessica gulped her milk. "Daddy, you have to listen to me."

"I'm listening."

"I didn't mean to make you scared. I didn't mean to make you mad. I wasn't running away. I was just trying to go someplace until Mom was gone for sure so I didn't have to leave you. Except then it started raining, and there was thunder so I hid. Only I wasn't hiding from you, so don't be mad—"

"I'm not mad, sweetheart."

"You're sure?"

"I'm sure."

"Then while you're not mad, could we talk about something else?"

"Anything you want." Simon wiped the milk smudge off her chin.

"Look, Dad, I have it all figured out. You marry Bree, and then we can all live here. Like a family. We'd be a family. And Mom can come and live with us, too. We have lots of room for her. We have lots of room for everybody...."

Bree suddenly discovered the dish soap suspended in her hand. The faucet was running, forgotten. Jessica was still running on, too.

"This is a good house. Everybody laughs in this house. You. Me. Bree. We're happy. We need this house, Dad."

Simon calmly coaxed his daughter into another spoonful of noodles. "Initially, I thought the idea was nuts, but I seem to have slowly come around to your way of thinking. If you want this house, we'll keep this house, lovebug. Okay?''

"Okay."

"But your mom and I don't live together anymore. I can't fix that, Jess."

"Okay."

"And we need to get something straight, short stuff. You worry if your mom is sad. You worry if you think I am. I want you to try and remember that we're the grown-ups. Grown-ups can take care of themselves. You don't have to worry about them."

"Okay."

The sink was starting to overflow. Bree hastily flipped off the tap and impatiently reached for a towel. Her heart was suddenly racing, racing. Only, she told herself, because he was so wonderful with Jess. He'd lost that lecturing tone and talked at her level now. He listened. And as Simon always had been and always would be, he was meticulously honest and careful not to make promises to Jessica that he couldn't keep.

"Okay," Jess echoed again, this time to a comment Bree had missed. "But what about—"

Simon's voice had lowered, quieted. It was almost inaudible from across the room. "I love you, Jess. You can count on that your whole life—it'll never change. But love between grown-ups is a different thing. I can't make Bree stay, honey. Not if she doesn't want to."

"But—"

The kitchen lights suddenly flickered, and then the room went black. Completely black as they lost power. Simon's response was not necessarily appropriate for a child's ears. Bree was standing frozen.

Only Jessica let out a thrilled, "Wow! Is this great or what?"

At ten-thirty that night, Bree pinned up her hair and stepped into the tub in the upstairs bathroom. The water was hot, softened with a little oil and scented with a few drops of perfume. She rested her neck against the cool porcelain edge and closed her eyes.

It had been an incredible day, starting with Liz's surprise arrival and continuing with Jess's disappearance. The power failure had only added to the confusion.

The storm had petered out shortly after dinner, but the power hadn't been restored until an hour ago. Even so late, Simon had his hands full coaxing Jessica into bed. Neither adult could worry that Jess suffered any repercussions from her little adventure in the storm. She had a wonderful time racing around the house with a flashlight, moaned vociferously when the lights went back on and complained, yawning, when Simon insisted on tucking her in.

Although the little one might not remember it, she went out faster than a knocked out prizefighter.

Bree smiled as she inhaled the fragrant steam. She'd been as physically wrung out as Jess before she stepped into the bath. Slowly, though, the hot soak was working its magic. Weightless, warm, her tired muscles gradually relaxed. Her heart stopped pumping like a jackhammer. Her mind cleared of distractions and was free to concentrate on what she'd wanted to all day.

Simon.

It was so easy, she thought, for a human being to temporarily lose his way. A person could be physically lost, as Jessica had been tonight in the Badlands. Or emotionally lost, the way Simon had been when she first met him, a sleepwalker, unconscious of his own loneliness except at some deep primal level.

Or a woman, Bree mulled, could be so afraid of hurt that she might temporarily lose all perspective and faith in herself.

She thought about the very first night Simon had stolen into her bed, how she had never felt threatened by him. She thought about how aggravatingly he had challenged her to relook at her life-style. She thought about all they had communicated in bed, not just desire but each other's most vulnerable needs. And she thought about his low, raw voice telling Jessica that he couldn't make her stay.

Simon loved her.

No one but a complete jerk could possibly judge his actions any other way.

I think this complete jerk's been in the tub long enough, don't you, Reynaud?

Bree stood up, flipped open the drain and reached for a towel. Her limbs were still a little lethargic, yet she moved quickly now, hurrying. She dried her legs, then whisked the towel across her back. The thick terry cloth caught at the clasp of her necklace. Even for a bath, she rarely removed the *maron*. The Cajun superstition had been ingrained since she was knee-high that the maran would always protect her from losing her way.

Now she slipped it off her neck and laid the talisman on the sink.

Still slightly damp, she reached for the pins on her head. Her hair uncoiled in a slow, tumbling mass,

tickling as it brushed her bare back. She neatly folded
the towel on the rack and silently turned the doorknob.

There was no sound on the second floor, and the air
was shivery cool on her bare skin. Jessica's door was
closed, but Simon's bedroom door, at the far end of
the hall, was slightly ajar. A rectangle of pale yellow
light streamed into the hall. He was reading, she
guessed, and she felt a feather of nerves raise goose
bumps on her skin.

She was sure of what she felt for Simon, but not so
sure of her plan. Her whole life she'd been a complete
disaster at planning anything to do with emotions. Yet
this was different. This was for Simon, and Simon
believed she was unwilling to be honest with him.

The truth that she'd blocked far too long was that
she was the real sleepwalker, a soul wandering lost
because she was too afraid to trust, too afraid to believe in a truly giving man even when she found him.

Bree intended to tell him. The words mattered. Yet
she sought a way to show him her heart—to offer her
heart—at a level that Simon could uniquely understand.

She took a huge breath. The stairs leading to her
third-floor tower room were located right next to the
bathroom. She walked past them and kept going.

Sitting on the corner of the bed, Simon tugged off
one sock, then the other. His eyes were full of tired
grit, his mood restless and edgy—not a winning frame
of mind to talk with Bree. It was going to happen.
Tonight. First, though, he was going to put his feet up
for an hour if it killed him. Tackling the Gypsy would

take finesse, understanding and patience. Right now, he was more in the mood to jam a ring on her finger, glue it there, and to hell with the finesse.

Morosely he tossed the socks in the corner, then pulled his shirt free from his pants. He was reaching for the first shirt button when he started having visions.

Granted, he was beat. Granted, his mind was on Bree. Granted, he had a slightly overactive subconscious when the sun went down, but at his worst, Simon had never been prey to having visions.

He groped behind him. His fingers connected with the paperback he'd planned to relax with, then they clawed further and grappled for his reading glasses. He slammed them onto his nose.

She was still there. Still standing naked in his doorway. A nymph from a man's fantasy, with lustrous dark hair swaying to her nipple tips and her skin heat buffed to a glow. Droplets of water still glistened in the dark triangle between her thighs, and her eyes had a glaze...a sultry, sloe-eyed, burning glaze.

If she trembled any harder, he thought, she was going to make herself ill. He forgot about ever feeling impatient with her. "Bree, honey..."

She didn't respond. At least verbally. Soundlessly, slowly, she crossed the room and deliberately removed the glasses from his nose.

The reading lenses were plunked onto a side table, his paperback pushed to the floor. He heard the thunk when the book landed, but he wasn't paying much attention.

Small white hands were climbing up his chest, slowly opening buttons in their wake. The third button caught on a thread. When it wouldn't immediately give, she tugged. The button arched across the room and hit the lamp shade with a ping.

His wanton seductress was too busy to notice. Simon figured the average earthquake wasn't likely to divert her attention. Bree was singularly focused, dead serious and determined. To please him. That kind of unbearable vulnerability was in her eyes.

"Sweetheart, you don't have to do this...."

Velvet fingertips tenderly traced his lips, wooing his patience. Her message was clear. She may not have to do this, but she wanted to. And that was the second time he noticed she hadn't spoken a word.

Simon could hardly miss the difference. All the other nights, Bree had talked. With words, she'd tried to reduce their lovemaking to a fantasy level. With words—he'd understood for some time—she had been fiercely, stubbornly determined to protect herself.

Not tonight. She climbed onto the bed, climbed onto him, and there was something naked in her eyes. Naked and soft and brave. Straddling his lap, she pushed the shirt off his shoulders inch by inch, lavishing every inch of his revealed skin with fervent, tender kisses. Loving kisses. There was probably nothing on earth sexier than loving kisses.

Simon would have wrapped her up and held her...only too late, he discovered himself trapped. She'd stripped the shirt off his torso, only the fabric was bunched where the sleeves were yet unbuttoned at the cuffs. She didn't seem aware that his arms were tangled in the sleeves, useless and immobile. She was concentrating too hard on taking his mouth.

It wasn't a kiss. It was a claiming, a wooing. A woman laying herself bare. Lips, warm and sweet, shivered over his, then molded, clung, promised, teased, took. Small fingers splayed, holding his head still, while her tongue dove inside his parted lips.

Bree quit breathing. He doubted Bree was aware she was rocking in his lap, friction rocking against his zipper, and her bare breasts were arched against his chest. He jerked at his hands, found them still trapped by the stupid cuff buttons and fleetingly swore to never again wear oxford shirts in this life.

As long as Bree was in his life.

And that was the first time Simon knew she would be. Whether she knew it, she was talking about her fears. They had nothing to do with sex, everything to do with vulnerability. His incorrigibly free spirit had the courage to take her own roads, an unquenchably giving nature and a reckless habit of putting everyone's needs before her own...but it was hard for Bree, very hard, to take the risk of losing.

She was taking that risk now. For him. Her eyes closed, fervent with emotion, they opened so he could see her expression. *I love you, Simon. With all my heart.* Eventually she figured out that she'd forgotten his shirt cuffs. Apparently she hadn't planned that, because her lips curled in a flash of feminine humor. Quickly she fingered loose the buttons, freed him of the shirt and then wound her arms around his neck again.

Only Simon figured it was about time he took a little control. She was already straddling his lap, so he hooked his arms under her hips and lifted her. If he'd ruined her mood, he was going to shoot himself, but it was necessary to walk over and close the door. Jess was sleeping, but she was still just down the hall. There was no way he wanted this night interrupted.

Neither did Bree. She realized where and why they were walking. With her lips molded to his, she reached out to blindly push the door. He just as blindly locked it.

When he carried her back to the bed, she landed with a little whoosh on the mattress. He pinned her securely and took advantage of his dominant position to nip the lobe of her left ear. "How long," he asked huskily, "have you had this sleepwalking problem?"

"Too damn long, Simon."

"It's the most vulnerable feeling on earth."

"Yes."

"At some unconscious level, you feel like you're searching...searching for something critically important to you. You're afraid you'll never find it."

"Yes."

"I found it with you, Bree. You're what I was looking for. I love you, sweetheart. And there's no way—*none*—I'd ever let you go."

"Simon," she said patiently, "you have this hopelessly confused. You're the stuckee in this scenario. Your first disastrous mistake was taking in a lost traveler in a storm. Your second was loving her in a way she never believed a man would love her. And when a man makes those kinds of mistakes, *cher,* he's simply stuck paying the price."

Damn him, he was smiling. Grinning like a self-satisfied smug devil was more like it. Possibly, she thought, he still didn't quite realize what she had in store for him.

She kissed him with methodical thoroughness, because Simon was definitely a man who appreciated methodical thoroughness, and then reached between them for his pants zipper. She slid the zipper down real slow. When that was done, she skipped her palms down his hips, down his thighs and calves, as she pushed off his jeans and underwear. The last of his clothes thunked on the floor.

"Bree—"

She heard him. He wanted her to come to him. She didn't have to seduce him; he was already seduced.

But seduction wasn't and never had been on her mind. Loving him was. Simon had taught her the dimensions of trust. She was determined to offer him the same gift. Control and self-discipline were integral to his character. When he lost both, she'd be there. For him. With him.

No one in this four-poster was wandering around nights alone anymore. She wanted to be sure he knew.

It was no simple job, sabotaging his control, submarining his self-discipline. It took an enormous amount of love and patience. She had to intuit where he wanted to be touched, where he needed to be touched. Simon was no help. He liked everything, and he kept looking at her with a steady, dark fire building in his eyes.

She used her hands, her tongue, her body to help him relax. Part of him did. Part of him hopelessly became more tense, so eventually she concentrated her efforts there. She explored, stroked, soothed, learned what pleased him with her fingertips. Then her tongue.

Until he swore. Loudly and rather dauntingly in French. Heaven only knew where he'd picked up all those dirty words and very bad grammar, but suddenly she found herself lifted, shifted and leveled flat on the mattress. "We'll have to work on your language," she murmured.

"Later."

"I want you," she said fiercely, "to feel loved."

"Which you've done, dangerously well. But right now I'm afraid we're going to have to concentrate completely on you, love."

He wrapped her legs around him and held her taut. She welcomed his slow, deep intrusion into the most intimate part of her, yet she thought she knew him well, thought she knew everything about the lover in Simon. He proved her wrong. The rhythm of love was familiar, but this was deeper, darker, sweeter magic. He loved her until she ached, until fire ripped through her, consuming, burning, until the only thing in her head was loving this man and being loved by him.

She soared so high that she thought she was lost. But he found her. He took her to a place of rainbows and wonder, a place where a woman was incomparably free, a place where fire was a soft, silver hush in her soul. The place was Simon's heart.

She'd come home.

In time, Simon found the energy to switch off the lamp. In the cool darkness, he tugged at the sheet and blankets until they were both under them instead of over them. Bree didn't help. She lay there like a repleted, sated, whipped-tired puppy, but Lord, those eyes.

"You do realize," she murmured teasingly, "that this is going to be the first solid night's sleep I've had since I met you."

"You think it's the air in the Badlands?"

"I think it's a problem unique to falling in love with a sleepwalker." She nuzzled closer. "Almost from the first, I had this idea that your problem had a relatively easy solution. A woman. The kind of woman who would keep you so busy nights that you didn't have the energy left to sleepwalk."

"Anyone volunteering?"

"Not me. I'm too beat."

"Well, I could go looking for someone else—"

"You try it. I'd catch you before you even reached the door. You're mine, *cher*. And don't try to get out of any commitment because we're a little different in temperament."

"A *little* different?" He'd known for some time that she was a nightmare to keep covered. When she leaned over to kiss his throat, the blanket slipped off her shoulder. Again.

"That's what I thought at first . . . until I realized how fundamentally we're alike. We both take care of people. We've both been lost. Really lost. We have the same kind of scars, Simon, and at the heart level we have the same kind of needs. To find someone we can trust, absolutely. Love, absolutely. Feel secure enough to change and grow and learn with, absolutely."

"It took you a while to figure that out, Reynaud."

"I thought you were going to kick me out."

"You're not very smart."

"I found you, didn't I?"

"All right. You're reasonably smart."

"Smarter than you, Courtland," she assured him. "I had the good sense to love you first."

He gave up trying to keep her covered. There was really only one thing to do with Bree when she was in this sassy frame of mind. She seemed unsurprised when he tucked her beneath him, nicely pinned her hands and tried—it was a good try—to kiss her quiet.

"I was kind of hoping you might want to talk about . . . weddings. Babies. Plans."

"I do." Lord, those eyes. So full of love. He'd never imagined that much love, not that belonged to him. "Later."

*   *   *   *   *

Silhouette Special Edition

proudly presents
the long-awaited "prequel" volume of

★ LOVE AND GLORY ★

by
LINDSAY McKENNA
Dawn of Valor

In the summer of '89, Silhouette Special Edition premiered three novels celebrating America's men and women in uniform: LOVE AND GLORY, by bestselling author Lindsay McKenna. Featured were the proud Trayherns, a military family as bold and patriotic as the American flag—three siblings valiantly battling the threat of dishonor, determined to triumph . . . in love and glory.

Now, discover the roots of the Trayhern brand of courage, as parents Chase and Rachel relive their earliest heartstopping experiences of survival and indomitable love, in

Dawn of Valor, Silhouette Special Edition #649

This month, experience the thrill of LOVE AND GLORY—from the very beginning!

Available at your favorite retail outlet, or order your copy by sending your name, address, zip or postal code, along with a check or money order (please do not send cash) for $2.95, plus 75¢ postage and handling, payable to Silhouette Reader Service to:

In the U.S.
3010 Walden Ave.
P.O. Box 1396
Buffalo, NY 14269-1396

In Canada
P.O. Box 609
Fort Erie, Ontario
L2A 5X3

Please specify book title with your order. Canadian residents add applicable federal and provincial taxes.

 *Silhouette Books*®

DV-1A

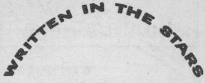

WRITTEN IN THE STARS

**Star-crossed lovers?
Or a match made in heaven?**

Why are some heroes strong and silent ... and others charming and cheerful? The answer is WRITTEN IN THE STARS!

Coming each month in 1991, Silhouette Romance presents you with a special love story written by one of your favorite authors—highlighting the hero's astrological sign! From January's sensible Capricorn to December's disarming Sagittarius, you'll meet a dozen dazzling and distinct heroes.

Twelve heavenly heroes ... twelve wonderful Silhouette Romances destined to delight you. Look for one WRITTEN IN THE STARS title every month throughout 1991—only from Silhouette Romance.

STAR

Silhouette Books®

SILHOUETTE·INTIMATE·MOMENTS®

WELCOME TO
FEBRUARY FROLICS!

This month, we've got a special treat in store for you: four terrific books written by four brand-new authors! From sunny California to North Dakota's frozen plains, they'll whisk you away to a world of romance and adventure.

Look for

L.A. HEAT (IM #369) by Rebecca Daniels
AN OFFICER AND A GENTLEMAN (IM #370) by Rachel Lee
HUNTER'S WAY (IM #371) by Justine Davis
DANGEROUS BARGAIN (IM #372) by Kathryn Stewart

They're all part of February Frolics, available now from Silhouette Intimate Moments—where life is exciting and dreams do come true.

FF-1A

 Silhouette Books®

SILHOUETTE·INTIMATE·MOMENTS®

NORA ROBERTS
Night Shadow

People all over the city of Urbana were asking, Who was that masked man?

Assistant district attorney Deborah O'Roarke was the first to learn his secret identity . . . and her life would never be the same.

The stories of the lives and loves of the O'Roarke sisters began in January 1991 with NIGHT SHIFT, Silhouette Intimate Moments #365. And if you want to know more about Deborah and the man behind the mask, look for NIGHT SHADOW, Silhouette Intimate Moments #373, available in March at your favorite retail outlet.

NITE-1

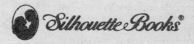

Silhouette Books®